GW01458071

Hi!

I hope y

love Phoebe x

POINT OF VIEW
It's all relative, really

PHOEBE WILBY

Published by

Delahoyde Publishing Company Limited

First Published September 2015

Text & Graphic Copyright © Phoebe Wilby, 2015

Wilby, Phoebe

Point of View: It's all relative, really

Paperback Edition

ISBN 978-0-473-33203-7

**Contact Phoebe Wilby at Delahoyde Publishing Co Ltd at
Info@DelahoydePublishing.com**

DEDICATION

To my Mum,
Without whose love and support, I am nothing.

Table of Contents

ACKNOWLEDGMENTS

Getting a book ready for publication is a hard slog,
and I certainly couldn't have done it alone. My family
have supported my efforts and provided the
inspiration.
Thank you for bearing with me and encouraging me.

SHORT STORIES

PHOENIX

There is non-seasonal rain. Thunder rumbles and lightning splits the clouds into streaks of silver, black and grey. It is a perfect day for a funeral. A classic; the weather I always imagine for my own funeral. It seems fitting to herald David's curtain-call with such inclement weather. It pleases me, though not obviously, I hope.

I feel cool and stylish and know I look attractive in my mourning dress. Black is my favourite colour. Today is the perfect day to show off my new outfit. I love it. The veil covers my face and drapes over my shoulders in deep cascades of cool, black chiffon, totally covering my hair. I hide behind it. The unnatural stoop of my shoulders, however, now bowed in grief and mourning, cannot be disguised by the veil, nor can the thin, black gauze hide the trembling in my hands and the unsteadiness of my gait. Yet, I play my part to perfection.

They're holding the service in the little chapel in the centre of the graveyard. The celebrant is wearing a black suit adorned with a flowery cravat and kerchief. Very, um, nice. (That celebrants conduct funerals is a new one on me. I thought they were the domain of the marriage ceremony.) Bright flowers cascade over the casket and beautiful bouquets adorn every pew. The organ music softly plays some unfamiliar hymns but the overall feeling is one of well-being. I feel at peace, knowing David is getting the well-staged farewell he deserves.

Friends and family fill the little chapel to capacity. The numbers surprise me, as I had no idea David had so large a family or that he was so popular. In all the years I knew him, I had met few of his friends and because of the distance, his family was a shadow in the background. It pleases me to see so many people there. I feel a little awkward, however, and somehow out of place. This is so unlike me, as I enjoy the opportunity to perform.

The service starts promptly. Idly, I wonder how many more funerals the celebrant will perform today. I read somewhere that every second, two people die at some place in the world. The odds are there are many people being buried today. Some of those people must have died around here, and they will probably also be buried today. A marriage celebrant shares a family's joy. A funeral celebrant shares their grief and sorrow. It takes a special person to officiate at funerals.

"Dearly Beloved, we are gathered here today...." Is this a funeral or a wedding? " ... to join with family and friends of David Whittaker Caldwell in bidding David a final goodbye and God speed, as he concludes his journey throughout this life, and embarks on the next chapter of his eternal existence." Beautiful words. Borrowed from a priest, perhaps.

"Mrs Caldwell," the celebrant continues, "has requested that several of David's friends and family address us today, to speak to us about David, who he was and the person he was." I am looking forward to this. Do other people see David the same way I do? I think perhaps not. Ours was a special relationship. No other person on earth could have known David the way I knew him. The first person to speak is David's brother, Mark. I knew Mark. He is ten years older than David and his hero. Mark could do no wrong in David's eyes. How did Mark feel about David?

"David was a special brother," began Mark, "too special for words." I had to agree with that. "When we were younger, David followed me everywhere - as younger brothers are apt to do. I was flattered at first, but as I reached my teens and other interests took my fancy," (a discreet cough here as he looked in the direction of a beautiful redhead I knew to be his wife), "I'm ashamed to say I neglected him. He was always in the way. I still loved him, though, and I hoped I showed him my feelings. As he grew into a young man, I watched the changes in him. He was always a loving person and these qualities grew and magnified as he grew. By the time he reached his early twenties, he was surrounded by friends and acquaintances vying for his attention. No matter how busy he was, he always found time for his friends."

I knew him as a loving person, too. I wonder to what changes Mark refers.

"When David married, I worried that he would suffer from burn out. Now he would have to devote time to one special person and I wasn't sure he was prepared for that. Yet it appeared my fears were ungrounded as his was a happy marriage. I'm sure Candice can vouch for that. It wasn't until much later David began to suffer. I hope and pray no other human will need to suffer as he did."

Suffer? Mark knew? I thought only I saw David's suffering. He was always cheerful around other people. Mark concludes his little speech by addressing David - or at least - the coffin.

"David, Mate. I'm going to miss you. You never knew it, and I never told you, but you inspired many of us to keep going, even when everything was stacked against you. I hope you're at peace now. I know you are and hope we'll meet again. If I can be half the man you were, I know we'll meet again." *David was twice the man you are*, Mark, I say to myself. *He was perfect.*

Joanie Dickson nee Anderson, apparently an old school friend of David's, is next. She stands tall and graceful in beautiful black georgette with gold buttons. Her blond hair matches the buttons with shine and falls in soft waves about her shoulders, framing an impishly cute face. Very stylish. Very beautiful. I feel the old surge of jealousy pull at my heart. Joanie is still such a beautiful woman. No woman can ever hope to compete with her sophistication. I am yet to meet her - having only seen her from a distance - but I always envied her poise and grace. I wonder if I look as good as she does. Her memories of David are as the good friend he had been to countless students.

"David really cared, and to see so many of his old friends here today proves that we all cared in return." Her words drip from her lips, saccharin sweet. "He was special - really something else. If any of the girls had no date for the formal, he would often take them along, too, or at least offer to dance a few numbers with them. Not many guys would do that, but David never baulked at showing a little kindness, even to the less than popular. I would often see a group of plain-looking girls surrounding David. He made them feel special." I am sure she was never dateless on a Friday or Saturday night. I remember she was always one of the first to be asked to dance at the school dances. It would seem easy to be happy with David's acts of kindness when you weren't in need of them yourself!

"David," she concluded, "I hope you will continue to be the sweet, caring man in your new life as you always were here with us. I firmly believe that life simply doesn't end at death. It continues forever in some form or another. If this is true, then you will be always alive. In fact, if it's true, I have no need to speak of you as a deceased person. Your body is decaying, but your soul is alive. You are still you. We just can't see you any more. Please remember us all, and look after us. We all need a Guardian Angel. You were one in life: I know you'll be one in death. Till we meet again, David. Farewell."

Joanie gently sponges some tears away from her carefully made up eyes, sniffs delicately, steals a final, yearning look at the flower-adorned coffin, and resumes her seat in a pew in the middle of the chapel. I don't know how I should take her little speech. What does she really feel for David? I cannot help feeling Joanie's words are all an act, a mere show. Perhaps I am being a little harsh. After all, people deal with grief in many different ways. I could be seeing Joanie's grief displayed in a most unusual way. She never was one to display emotion of any sort. I believe that was why most of the girls at school had avoided her; and perhaps the very quality which drew the boys to her, like ants to honey.

I wonder how Candice is holding up and allow my eyes to wander over the congregation until they rest on her. From my chosen seat at the back of the chapel, I can see her sitting ramrod-straight in the front pew, apparently staring at the coffin. Her shoulders are rigid - not the carefree, relaxed woman I remembered from my youth. She is beautiful, just like Joanie, but more refined and pure. Finding adequate words to describe Candice is very difficult. I have known her for many years, yet her beauty is still breathtaking.

She is raven-haired, tall and slender without being

too thin. Well shaped is probably a better way to describe her figure. Her face, now covered by the veil, is only gently lined and these lines add a depth to her beauty. She is a mysterious woman; very difficult to understand. David was never attracted solely to beauty and many people wondered what David had seen in her. But I knew. Nobody knows David the way I know him! My wandering attention is brought back to the service by the intonation of the celebrant.

"David was much loved by all who knew him, as our two previous speakers have noted. Mrs Caldwell has requested that a work colleague, Peter Beaumont, now address us."

This is a surprise. I know Peter Beaumont. He and David have never agreed on a business deal. What could Peter possibly say about David? I hoped he had the common sense not to rail David in front of the entire congregation, as he was accustomed to doing in board meetings. I shudder as I watch Peter's heavy frame advance to the podium. I steal another quick glance in Candice's direction. She remains rigid and unmoving. What is she thinking of? How can she ask David's arch enemy to speak at his funeral? I am terrified he will say the wrong thing. My fears proved ungrounded. True, his words took on double meaning when the extent of the rivalry between him and David was known. However, I believe that, with the possible exception of Candice, I am the only person here besides Peter himself who knows that.

"David was a most remarkable business man," he

begins. "To work with him was a real challenge as he always expected the best of himself and his colleagues. I believe he did in death what he always preached in life. He did the best he possibly could." What is that supposed to mean? Did he expect David to die more spectacularly than he has?

".... David was a perfectionist. He lived the perfect life; married the perfect woman; raised perfect children; performed perfectly at work and in the end, he died perfectly, too. He died as we all would want to: without fuss or panic. David, continue your perfect life wherever it may take you. There is a hereafter, I firmly believe that; a perfect hereafter for you."

There isn't a dry eye in the chapel after Peter's speech. Peter can always do that. He has missed his vocation - should have gone on the big screen. I don't like Peter, though for David's sake, I tolerate him. He is a brilliant business man - even David admitted that - but he lacks ethics. He rides roughshod over every colleague; what friends he has are wary of him. However, every client applauds him. To them there is no better, so while David did the ground work and the behind-the-scenes slog, Peter grandstanded on centre stage. It appears to me he has even managed to overshadow David's funeral.

I expect Candice to say some words but she is obviously too stressed to face the crowd. I don't mind. I could say something, though I doubt it is appropriate for me. My relationship with David, how we met, the antics we used to get up to, the type of man I found David to be will not be discussed publicly. The celebrant announces the end of the service with a beautiful hymn - one I am familiar with and he then says a final prayer. It is all very moving and lovely. I nearly cry myself, but I've better control of myself than that.

David's body is to be interred underneath an old river gum in the centre of the cemetery, not far from the little chapel. The guests file out of the chapel, following Candice in a solemn line. Mark holds a large, black umbrella over Candice to shield her from the torrential rain. She seems unaware of his presence, or even of the rain and Mark has to follow her lead to keep her from becoming wet.

I follow behind the crowd, wanting to remain invisible. My own black umbrella is larger than usual and I am reminded of an old nursery rhyme about a big, black umbrella crossing a street on a misty, moisty morning. I stand at the extreme back of the group, craning my neck to see better. It was essential for me to make sure David made it into his grave, yet I hoped for anonymity. Some morbid part of me expects David to rise from his grave and say it was all a big joke. You know. 'Thanks for coming and all that. Good to see you all cared, but it's time to go home now, folks,' that sort of thing. I don't want that to happen, of course, but something just seems not quite right somehow. I feel an absurd desire to burst into hysterical laughter well up inside me that I somehow manage to quell.

The little procession, diminished by the rain, reaches the grave side. Rain has formed miniature rivers of red mud running down the excavation mounds and into the prepared pit. Terrifying visions come to me of the pallbearers slipping in the mud and landing on the bottom of the pit, with the coffin on top of them. That would certainly put an end to the perfect funeral - a not-so-perfect end to David's perfect life. However, nothing of that type happens - much, I presume, to Candice's relief. And mine. Hysteria would break out then!

The celebrant speaks a few more words over the grave, the coffin is lowered and the first clod of dirt is dropped on top of it. Candice, her eyes still expressionless, drops a single red rose into the grave, and then turns away. She glances in my direction, and for one horrifying moment, I think she's seen me. I hold my breath as her incredibly blue eyes, now shielded by the black veil, hold mine. There is no spark of recognition and I slowly expel my breath as she walks to the waiting limousine without a backwards glance.

I feel a little sorry for David in that moment. When I die, I hope my loved ones will weep at my grave side for me. Surely that would be a sign of respect and love. Then again, I could be judging Candice as harshly as I may have judged Joanie. And my own eyes have remained dry throughout the whole service.

It was Candice and not I who dealt with David's

growing stress. Candice comforted David when the strain of living up to perfection finally became too much. Candice, not I, encouraged David to stand up to Peter Beaumont and expose him for the charlatan he is. And Candice found David at the end, a worn-out shell of the man he used to be. She, not I, is burying her husband and is entitled to display her grief in whatever way is best for her. She loved David at least as much as he loved her. I'm sure.

The rest of David's family stays behind at the grave. No one speaks, and no one cries, yet emotion is evident on all their faces. Each member drops roses or petals on the coffin. Of all the family, only Mark appears calm and in control of his emotions. Speaking during the service would have helped tremendously. Dealing with grief is never easy - or predictable.

Roses and rose petals totally cover the lowered coffin by now. The original flowers adorning the coffin have long since been removed. I presume they are on their way to various homes to brighten the drab abodes on this dark and dismal day. I didn't see Candice take any, though there could have been a bouquet or two in the limousine. I wonder if a gathering, a wake of sorts, has been planned. If so, no one appears too anxious about leaving. Only Candice has left the cemetery. Friends and family mill in their separate groups, discussing David's death, the funeral, or perhaps it was the weather. I begin to feel a little conspicuous, having attached myself to no particular group, and indeed, belonging to none.

As nonchalantly as I can, I slip back to the chapel. There is an "In Memoriam" visitors' book for guests to sign as a remembrance for David's family of those who attended the funeral. I have a wicked thought that perhaps I should sign it, too, but I'm sure the joke would not be appreciated by Candice. I have no intention of hurting her. If she recognised me at the funeral, she made no sign. Perhaps she had no desire for unpleasant scenes either. I scan the names on the attendance list and am astonished to discover five pages of neatly scrawled names. I didn't realise the chapel could accommodate so many! David would be pleased.

By now, the crowd has begun to disperse and I begin to feel more comfortable. I am satisfied David's send-off has been to his liking. I am certainly pleased with it. I wait until the last guest departs. A lone black limousine with a liveried chauffeur stands at the far end of the car park under a tree. I gingerly make my way over to it, dodging stones and puddles as best I can. Stiletto heels are not made for terrain such as this! James, my chauffeur opens the rear door for me and helps me to enter.

"I trust the funeral was as well, er, executed as expected ... Ma'am," James questions. Our eyes meet in the rear vision mirror and I detect an unaccustomed glint in James' eyes.

"Just beautiful," I say. "I couldn't have planned it better myself."

I sit in the back of the limousine rubbing tired,

sore ankles. New shoes are always difficult to break in and these are particularly gruelling. I am so tired. It has been a hard day and I am ready for relaxation. It isn't over yet.

"Take me home, please, James."

The engine purrs as we pull out of the car park and ease into the afternoon traffic. There is a change of clothes hanging in the back. I am eager to rid myself of these glad rags. And the make-up! So thick and uncomfortable! Back in comfortable clothes again, I can offer a sigh of relief.

"Are you sure you haven't forgotten something?" James' question startles me out of a light nap. I look into the mirror and immediately see to what he refers.

"Ah, yes!" Gingerly, I bring my hand up to my forehead. With a flourish, I tear the hat and veil from my head. The mane of flowing blond hair comes off at the same time, revealing a mass of short, unkempt chestnut curls. Much better.

"Candice will be expecting you soon. I'd better step on it." So saying, James enters the freeway, doubling his speed.

David's funeral was my idea although Candice planned it to perfection. What a woman! David was so lucky! Wait! I don't need to think of David like that anymore. The old David is gone, but *I'm* still alive. Candice and I can start a new life together, far away from the prying eyes of family and friends and the greedy, grasping fingers of commerce. There will be none to disturb the peace. My life insurance will see to it that we live in style!

I am David, and at last, I'm free.

RESOLUTION

It was late on New Year's Eve, a very bad time to shop.

Vanessa pushed the empty trolley to the nearest bay, a good 300 yards from where she had finally found a place to park her car two hours ago.

Her heels tapped a staccato beat as she strode along the pitted tarmac. It was bitterly cold; the wind bit through her faux-fur-lined winter coat, through the blazer, blouse and skirt and thick black tights which had become her corporate attire, through her pale, where-is-the-sun winter skin, right to the marrow of her bones. Chestnut hair was finally escaping from the tight roll she customarily wore and fine tendrils whipped her face and neck, stinging her exposed, chilled skin.

She'd had enough of crazed last-minute shoppers, vying for the last pomegranate, piece of pork, packet of grapes, bagels, whatever they felt would bring them luck for the New Year ahead. She only wanted to go home, curl up in front of the fire and forget about it all for the holidays. Vanessa sighed and shook her head in frustration, releasing another coiled strand. There was no rest for her at home.

She sighed as she pushed her trolley into the end of the line of parked trolleys and extricated her token with gloved hands.

"Fumble fingers!" she muttered, searching the ground for the token which had so elegantly slipped from her gloved fingers to the tarmac below. It didn't help that the token was a dull grey colour, and with the poor lighting, rendered almost invisible. Still, she hoped to catch a glimpse of its dull sheen – or at the very least, a coin-shaped shadow.

Miracle! She found it! She bent to retrieve it and was promptly rammed by a trolley.

"Oh! For goodness sake!" Teetering on high heels, she lost balance and fell on to the trolley, catching her face on the way down.

"I am so sorry!" His warm, liquid voice, contrite and apologetic, cut through her chilled brain. "Here, let me help you." And as she made to resist, "Can I at least take you to the light, make sure my absent-minded clumsiness hasn't caused any damage?"

She would have snapped at him, but something in his voice triggered a memory of happier, warmer days, and so she allowed him to lead her back to the light.

"Here. Let me see." Surprisingly gentle, warm fingers sent a blast of heat through her frozen body as he tilted her face to the light, blinding her, and so she missed the startled expression on her rescuer's face.

However, she didn't miss the quick intake of breath and she stared up into his face. It was in shadow, the golden halo around his head preventing her from defining his features.

"Is it bad?" she asked, her voice catching a little as she feared the worst.

"Nessie...?"

She froze, a rabbit caught in headlights, heart pounding, breathless.

"Kevin..." she exhaled, remembering to breathe in.

"It's been so long..."

"Twenty years... more..."

"That long?"

"You didn't write..."

"My mum said you'd left a message ... Didn't want me to."

"I wrote..."

An accusation left hanging...

"I moved..."

An awkward pause...

"Can I buy you a drink? We can catch up."

Hopeful.

"I have to get home. My husband... kids..." Her voice trailed off and she lowered her eyes, the only part of her body she still controlled.

"Of course. How insensitive of me." Still he held her chin, gently. Caressingly. Playing her. His touch awakened dormant thoughts and feelings which flowed through her deadened body, threatening to erupt in a symphonic explosion.

"Just ... ok..." She caught her breath as his lips brushed hers, warming her, yet sending delicious shivers through her body. She trembled uncontrollably. His warm breath stroked her lips inches from her own as his ocean-blue eyes held her hazel ones. Questioning. Promising.

Kevin smiled, the slow, easy smile she remembered, and released her chin, capturing her shoulders. He led her to the Hog's Head, powerless as a lamb to the slaughter.

"Kevin, maybe I should just..." Her voice trailed off.

The Hog's Head was crowded. He led her through the throng to a private booth. Tenderly, he eased her coat from her shoulders, taking her blazer with it, revealing her cream satin blouse. His fingers lingered at the nape of her neck and she demurely bowed her head, allowing the sweet contact. He eased the pins holding her hair, releasing chestnut waves. He twirled one curl and gently scraped the back of his hand across her cheek. She gasped at the intimate contact, but made no objection, and as he held her close, she hardly dared to breathe.

He smiled his slow, sweet smile again, and settled her in the booth. He left to get their drinks, but was not gone very long before she realised he hadn't asked her what she wanted. It didn't matter. She wouldn't be staying. She should be making final preparations for her family's New Year's celebrations – a quiet night at home, bringing in the New Year. She shouldn't be spending any time with Kevin, the man who broke her heart.

I'll go home now, she thought, and would have, except Kevin had returned.

"Do you still not drink?" he asked, placing a tumbler of tonic water in front of her.

She nodded, but at this moment wished for a triple vodka.

He sipped his cider appreciatively, sighing with contentment.

"The years have been kind to you," he said, eyes holding hers captive.

She blushed, and hoped the dim light hid it. From the sudden glint in his eye she guessed not, and felt herself blushing harder.

"You look well, yourself," she countered as lightly as she could, noting the still thick, dark, wavy hair now growing silver at the temples. Laughter lines made his already handsome face even more so. Another errant thought that sent the heat roaring through her body, suffusing her face with colour.

"Marriage suits you." It was designed to quell the fires burning in her body and came out frostier than intended.

He looked at her.

"My wife passed away five years ago. Cancer."

"I'm so sorry." Vanessa bit her lip. An awkward silence developed. The knowledge that he was single again reinforced to her that her old feelings for him had not gone completely.

"How is … your husband? Kids?"

"I have three, girls, all in secondary now."

"I bet they're all as beautiful as you are."

"I think they're beautiful. They look like their…" She paused. "My … husband, Andrew … had an accident a few years ago. It was… I, er…," she sighed. "He's paralysed."

"That must be difficult." He watched her for signs that she would welcome his comfort. Once she would have allowed him to take over, but it seemed the years, although physically kind to her, had dealt her an emotional blow.

She toyed with her glass, moistening her finger

21

and rubbing it gently along the top edge. A sweet note erupted. She looked up at him. A sweet sadness reflected in her eyes, a sadness he could suddenly understand as the anguish of their separation erupted in his heart.

"I'm so sorry I didn't keep in touch." He hadn't meant to say it, but now he found he had no control over his mouth. He had loved his wife, after a fashion, but even she had known he still carried a torch for Vanessa.

"It was for the best. I would've held you back."

He could see she meant it.

"Vanessa, I..."

"Kevin, we..."

"You go first...," Kevin gestured for her to continue, and once again she found herself at a loss.

"This wasn't such a good idea, us having a drink." And then the words just tumbled out. "I appreciate you had your career to think of. I'm so happy to know you've made it. You're a fantastic musician, Kevin. I've always loved your music. I still have the first song you ever recorded for me – I had it put on a CD."

He stared at her, eyes suddenly stinging with unshed tears. He blinked away the threatened deluge, swallowing hard.

"I can make you another. Many more. All your old favourites. And my new ones. I'll write one ... just for you..."

"No!" Then more gently, "That would be lovely..."

Another awkward silence. Vanessa's finger still traversed the glass rim. Kevin stared at her, eyes dark with emotion. Suddenly, Vanessa looked directly at him.

"Why didn't you call, Kevin?" All the hurt of the past years pooled in her eyes; he found the haunted expression on her face unbearable.

"I was weak." His soft answer was almost lost in the general hubbub of the pub and she leaned forward to hear his response. "We were young, Vanessa. You were studying business; I was off to the Conservatorium; different goals; I didn't want to hold you back." *Mum didn't want you to hold me back.*

His voice cracked. She didn't hear. She was nineteen again, standing under the ancient oak with him. He was holding her tight, promising to write, telephone, pop down for the weekend; promising they would spend vacations together; promising they had a future. They had clung to each other, seeking and giving reassurance. Their final kiss was full of passion. She still felt it. It still hurt.

"I really need to be getting home."

"I know."

He helped her into her blazer and coat.

"I'd like to see you again... Please?"

She looked into his face, searching, longing; finding. She leaned forward and kissed him gently on his cheek, tasting the salt, knowing her own face was wet, too.

"I'll always love you, Kevin." Her voice broke as she turned away. He held her arm to stop her.

"Vanessa, I... It wasn't a mistake. And it wasn't coincidence. Fate brought me here tonight."

"Shhh..." She held a warm finger to his lips. "Andrew needs me." She gave him a tight hug, clinging. He hugged her back. She turned to go before she changed her mind. Her loveless marriage would have been long over if Andrew hadn't had his accident, but how could she abandon him? Kevin still held her tight.

"I'll be waiting, Nessie," he whispered.

"Don't," she whispered back, heartbroken again.

He stared into her eyes, willing her to stay. Nothing, except the resolution to do her duty.

Slowly Kevin released his hold, watching as she turned and walked away.

***

The light dusting of snow that had fallen while she lingered with Kevin had deepened and was even now falling heavier, obliterating her tyre tracks. She parked her car in the garage and brought her shopping in, putting it straight away effectively delaying the meeting with her family. Through the glass, she watched while they sat, peaceful, in the front room.

Would they even know if I wasn't here?

She sighed, pasted a smile on her face and opened the door.

"Mummy!" Three voices in unison, pleased to see her, leapt up to welcome her with a hug. She swallowed the sudden lump in her throat as she hugged them back. Lovingly.

"Hello, Dear. Long day?" Andrew's frosty tones coming from his customary place on his recliner broke the happy reunion. She looked at him, trying to reconcile her decision to stay.

"I ran into an old friend at the PriceSave," she answered. "We had a drink and reminisced on old times. Sorry. Dinner won't be long."

She squared her shoulders and set to work assigning simple tasks to the children as they prepared their New Year feast. It would be a spectacular dinner, one to bring in the New Year with cheer. This New Year's Eve would herald the best year ever. She would make it so.

After the children had gone to their rooms and she had settled Andrew for the night, she sat alone in her room, listening to Kevin playing some music as he transported her away, at least in her mind.

WINTER INTERLUDE

It's early in the afternoon of a winter holiday. The sun is glorious though a little hot out of the wind. It's a little on the chilly side in the shade. We're having a bit of one-on-one time, my youngest daughter and I. We've decided to spend our time at the park at the end of our street. It's a wide expanse of gentle green hills with a few forest trees dotted here and there. Right on the edge in a pool of bark is a set of swings and a plastic, climbing contraption with a slide.

We take the cross-country option as Rachel heads for a small ditch rather than the stone strategically placed as a natural bridge further along. This is the first tumble of our outing and it's the beginning of her parkland adventure!

She heads straight for the swings and if she was a little taller, she would have climbed right up. No matter. I lift her up and fasten the safety chain. I push her gently and her eyes light up with the sheer joy of freedom. Only a persistent cough mars her joy.

Rachel has yet another coughing fit as her little body struggles with her fourth bout of the 'flu this year. She's had so many we can only let her ride it out. She forgets about her cough as a noise grabs her attention. She looks up and points.

"What's that?" I ask her.

"A plane!" she answers in her own language of barely discernible English.

She is growing up, but is still just a baby. She's not yet two, but so advanced for her age. With three older brothers and an older sister, it's no wonder. Sometimes I mourn her rapid advancement. She's growing up too fast.

Her light brown curls shine in the sunlight where the light turns them golden, and the joy of life shines from her dark brown eyes. She has an expressive elfin face with gorgeous dimples in her cheeks and upper lip and an open grin. She's a happy child and always a pleasure to have around.

She loves the swing and from watching those who know, she is learning to thrust her body backward and forward in an attempt to swing herself. There is not quite enough force in her thrusts yet. That will come with time. She loves to swing, but is forever tempted by the new plastic contraption consisting of chain ladder, rope, pole, steps, steering wheel, a couple of platforms and a slide, so she divides her time between the two.

She climbs up the steps, stomps and splashes in the puddle on one of the platforms, and pretends she is driving a car on the other. Sliding quickly down, she lands with a thump on her bottom, laughs joyously, and jumps up to repeat the cycle. She attempts to climb the chain rope but finds it too hard, preferring either the steps or to try to climb up the slide the wrong way. She's nearly inexhaustible, with boundless energy despite her current illness.

Back on the swing, she wants me to push her higher. As she swings back to me, I move my whole body closer, our faces mere inches apart. She thinks we're going to 'bang heads' but we miss and the nearness of the miss thrills her. Giggling uncontrollably, she almost falls off, but I catch her just in time. Then she laughs even harder. Daredevil!

I sit on the swing next to her and try to recapture my own childhood. I used to love the swing and would spend hours soaring through the air. I used to love roller coasters, too, and similar fairground attractions, but now find them all nauseous. I don't let her know this, though.

She becomes impatient with me. I am forever scribbling in my notebook, immortalising memories to be savoured in later years. I should have done this with all my children, but my efforts have always been haphazard and disorganised. Perhaps it will be different now.

A morning spent painting has left its mark on her.

There are colourful streaks on the backs of her hands and all over her oldest clothes. There is even a dark smudge on her right cheek and one on her left eyebrow. She's a little artist in embryo. Now she's outside in the park, splashing in the puddles on the platforms of the plastic plaything, scuffling through the bark under the swings, and landing on her bottom in the dirt at the end of the slide. She's having fun.

"Come on, Mum," she calls to me, and leads me back to the swing. Again. I would tire of it if I thought it would last forever, but I know it won't. She's my baby, the youngest of five. Sometimes I've been impatient to see them all grow up. Sometimes I still catch myself feeling that way, but then I remember they grow up so fast.

I follow her as she wanders off down the hill. She has had enough now, and is ready to go home. Plodding down the hill, she trips on something and tumbles down. The grass is long and soft and she isn't hurt. She turns to look at me and sits there for a little while, the sun creating a halo about her head, waiting for me to catch up. The grass almost hides her and she looks just like a mischievous elf in the woodlands. Then she jumps up and runs ahead of me once more.

She comes to the road and again waits for me to catch up. She doesn't usually do this but today she does. I offer her my hand, which she takes and we cross the road together. Climbing the final hill home is no ordeal. It isn't always like this. Usually she wants me to carry her. I'm grateful she's happy to walk today. I wonder how she's feeling, if she has enjoyed our few short minutes alone. Then she sees her big sister and brothers and runs towards them.

I have enjoyed this brief interlude with my youngest daughter. They happen rarely and are moments to cherish. It's over for now. She's gone on to play with the rest of them and I am left to go inside alone.

Point of View: It's all relative, really

THE TELEGRAM

It came with the morning post. Elizabeth knew the time was near. She had been expecting it for months now, ever since John joined the army. Still, she couldn't bear to open it. John was her life. He was her only son, her only child. Everything she did revolved around him. She loved him dearly. Why did he have to join the army? His father and grandfather had both been well-respected army officers. They had both died serving their country. Now John had gone away, too. He was part of the United Nations peace-keeping force in the Middle East. Peace! Why send an army to keep peace? Those Arabs knew nothing of peace! The Israelis were the same. Their soldiers were only children, but oh, they were seasoned. Real professionals. Now John had been sent there to keep the peace among them!

John was a good-looking lad - tall like his father and stocky like his grandfather, a real beast of a boy.

Well, a man really, though only just. He turned twenty-one today. He had thick, curly, black hair and blue eyes; and his skin tended to tan rather than freckle. His mouth was wide and generous, forever smiling. He had such courage and always faced his battles with a smile. At least, Elizabeth had always known him to.

She stood by the window, thinking back over the past twenty-one years. First, there was the day they had brought him home from the hospital. He was such a tiny lad, and it was so long ago. She seemed to remember that he was even smiling then, at only ten days old. Of course there were times during his boyhood when tears replaced his smile. Like the day he came off his pony, breaking his arm. Even then, he had been cheerful during the six weeks his arm was in plaster. Elizabeth didn't think John knew how to be sad for very long.

He turned ten just before they received word his father had died. Though John cried for a while, he bounced back faster than most to bear the responsibilities of the man in the house. Perhaps it did not seem fair to him. She may have expected too much of him - yet John shouldered his increased responsibility like a man. He never complained, but was always smiling. If he ever resented it, he never spoke of it to her.

When at sixteen, all his friends were intent on going out and doing their own thing, John never suggested doing likewise. He seemed to enjoy the company of his mother. The only thing he ever insisted on doing against her will was to join the Army. He knew she never wanted him to, but felt it was his duty. It was as though he could hear the call of the blood of his father and grandfather to take up arms to defend the right. John felt all men should fight for their country. He was a man therefore he should fight. So he enlisted, did his basic training and not long after, was sent to the Middle East.

He wrote often, but Elizabeth would receive nothing from him for months. Then four letters would arrive at once. They never really told her anything. She supposed it was because of censorship. Usually they would contain the same banal comments about the weather, the endless sand, and how tired he was, always ending with, "I love you, John." It had been four months since she'd heard from him, and now this.

Idly she bent down to pick up the envelope, turning it over and over in her hands as she sank heavily into the nearest seat. She remembered the time her mother had received an envelope just like this one.

"Lieutenant Johnson reported missing in action," it read. Shortly afterwards, she had received a detailed letter from the General's Aide recounting in cold clinical terms the events surrounding her husband's disappearance. His body was never recovered.

Eleven years ago, a similar envelope had arrived for Elizabeth. Except for her, there was to be no hope.

A small parcel of her husband's belongings had later arrived in the post, ending all possible reasons for hope. With it was a letter he had never sent. She still had it, along with everything else, locked away out of sight, but never out of mind. She had not looked at the letter since, but its content was etched in her heart, for that is where her love for him lay, even now. It read:

"My Darling Libby,

Here I am in this God-forsaken corner of the world wondering if I'm ever to see your beautiful face again. I sometimes wish I'd never heard of the Army. Life here is hell. I want nothing more than to be home with my family, my darling wife, and my darling son.

I'm due for leave soon. They'll be sending me home for a month or two for some R & R. Then it'll be back here, or perhaps somewhere worse.

Libby, darling, you'll never know what war does to a man. I hope you'll always remember that I love you and John with all my heart. I look forward to feeling your tender embraces again.

Yours forever,

Charles."

That was it but it was enough. She loved him then, and she loved him still. No one could ever replace him. She would never want anyone else.

The new envelope lay unheeded in her lap as tears

slipped from her eyes and slowly made their way down her cheeks. Her blue eyes were brighter than usual and her normally tanned face was pale and drawn. She seemed to have aged a lot in the time John had been away. She was still a beautiful woman but now, silver strands streaked her dark hair. Worry lines played havoc with her eyes and her lips were drawn in a perpetual look of determination. She supposed she should open the envelope but was reluctant to do so.

The thought of additional pain clutched at her heart-strings as she endeavoured to control the inevitable feeling of dread that invaded her very soul.

So the telegram lay, unopened in her lap as the last rays of daylight filtered through the curtains and the room began to darken. She could not have said how long she sat there like that. She only knew it was a long time.

A sharp rap on the door roused her from her reverie. Startled, she rubbed her eyes and forced her mind to take control of her weary body, to stop its senseless wanderings. As she stood, the envelope fluttered to the floor. Elizabeth never noticed.

Slowly, wearily, she made her way to the front door. She opened it. A handsome man wearing a tattered army uniform was standing on the doorstep, leaning on a crutch. His curly, dark hair needed trimming. His face was covered in stubble. There were heavy lines around his clear-blue eyes that had faded a little since she had last seen them. They sparkled with the perpetual smile they always wore.

"Elizabeth," he softly whispered.

Her face was an ashen mask as she stared at the apparition before her. In an act of self-preservation born of sheer necessity, she closed her tear-filled eyes, and when she opened them, he was still there.

"Charles," was all she said, as she took the man she once thought dead, her husband, into her warm embrace.

.

THE WEATHERMAN

"Raining?! You've got to be kidding me!"

Maddie stopped short as the sudden downpour caught her unawares a few paces on the outside of the automatic glass doors of the Student Services building. She cursed today's blue sky and sweltering heat that gave no clue to the downpour scheduled for this evening. She was late again as she so often was. And as he so often was, Jim was going to be mad.

She searched through her hold-all, hoping she had put an umbrella in, but no! Once again, she had left home without it, even though, due to the drought, the weatherman had promised the artificial rainfall every evening for a week, starting tonight.

"Saves on watering the garden, at least," Jim had said, his usual despondency lifting momentarily into sarcasm as he mocked the need for artificial rain. No one had a garden these days. There was no room for a garden in a city covered in concrete.

The rain replenished the city's water, and made everyone feel like they were living a normal life. It had not rained for days, weeks even, and so the weatherman decided that this week, they would have rain and so it was scheduled for 1900 hours.

Usually this would not have been a problem for Maddie, but tonight was the first night of the scheduled rain, and she was late.

"This should only last an hour or so," she muttered as she trudged back to the building. "Might as well sit it out in comfort."

The automatic door stood unyieldingly, ignoring her presence, refusing her entry. In frustration, she hammered on the glass, to no avail. It was after hours, and no one could get back in now.

Maddie resigned herself to a wet walk home. There was no shelter in that door-way, the glass opening flush with the building.

The streets were deserted. Most sane people had remembered the warning and were safely home. Not Maddie. Huge blobs of rain came thick and fast, soaking her thoroughly.

"Wish I'd worn something a little heavier," she mused, the thin white blouse and flowing trousers left nothing to the imagination. She might as well have been naked.

Maddie hurried down the alleys between the

buildings, hoping for some respite from the downpour which had steadily intensified until it resembled the heavy thunderstorms she remembered from her childhood.

She had been walking for half an hour before she realised she no longer knew where she was. Here the rain had been unable to wash away the city grime, and oily puddles marked her path. She had obviously taken a wrong turn somewhere in the dimly-lit alleys between the main thoroughfares. She had decided on the alleys because she knew there'd be no shelter along the main thoroughfares. Now she was faced with a blank wall. The buildings with their flush doors and grated fire escapes offered no respite from the downpour and the strong wind which had now arisen. Her saturated clothing and straggly wet hair whipped her. She was cold, miserable, lost, and, she was loathe to admit it, more than a little frightened.

There was nothing for it. She would have to go back the way she came, retrace her steps and hopefully find herself in more familiar surroundings. Eventually, she would find her way home.

At the alley entrance, she found she had three choices, although the third had not seemed an option before. She could go left which was the way she had just come, turn right which she hoped was towards home, or go straight ahead. The left and right turns were now in total blackness, but towards her, there was a glimmer of light spilling into the alley. It seemed that not all the citizens had barricaded themselves against the downpour, and with reckless resolution tinged with hope, Maddie cautiously made her way towards the light.

"'Ello, my lovely," the old crone held the lamp high, illuminating Maddie's glowing skin and noting the sandy, snake-like tendrils dripping water down her cheeks and back. "'Tis a poor night to be caught outside, innit?" she continued, grasping Maddie's arm with her bird-like claw and guiding her to the shelter.

It was not a home as Maddie had supposed, but a recessed doorway, its padlocked door barring entry to the building. However, the space offered some respite from the inclement weather.

"Thank you," Maddie managed a breathless reply to the old woman's kindness. She was too exhausted and cold to wonder why the old woman was outside herself on such a night as this.

Maddie hugged her arms to her chest, suddenly conscious of her transparent clothing, but the old dear drew a threadbare blanket from a dark corner of the recess and threw it over her shoulders, fashioning it into a cloak.

"Should take away some of the chill," she crooned, fussing around Maddie. "You'll soon be as good as new." She lapsed into a watchful silence, her dark, beady eyes never leaving Maddie's, boring into her soul.

It was surprisingly warm in the recess. Maddie supposed the wind which howled down the alley was too busy to find this corner. At any rate, she was grateful for the warmth.

"I should have left for home ages ago," Maddie said. The silence had become embarrassing now, and she shifted a little uncomfortably. Her legs, which had been numb from the cold, were now beginning to warm up, quite quickly, as it happened, and the tingling sensation as blood once again began to flow was a little uncomfortable.

"Did you not heed the weatherman's warning?" The old crone's tone was a little sharp.

"I didn't expect to be out so late."

Maddie stared at the curtain of water shielding the alley from her view.

"It should have been over by now. It usually only lasts an hour and I'm sure it's been more than that already."

The old lady remained silent for a moment, observing. She sighed.

"What brings you here, m'dear?" she finally asked.

"I was late leaving. I just stepped out and the rain started. No gentle mist gradually getting stronger like normal... it just bucketed down. I was soaked within seconds and tried to go back, but the door was locked. After hours, you see."

The old lady nodded. "You were warned, though. He warns everyone."

Maddie frowned. "Yes. This morning. On the

weather. The weatherman said it would rain at 1900 hours. I just forgot. Even forgot to pick up my umbrella."

"Yes. Still, you were warned."

"I suppose."

It had only been a few minutes and already Maddie was feeling toasty and dry. Cosy. She lifted the blanket and was surprised to find her clothes were dry, too.

"How is this possible?"

"Sorry?"

"I'm dry!"

"Yes..."

Maddie whirled to face the curtain of water cascading from the roof of the recess. "If I go out with this blanket, it will keep me dry!"

"It might... but I can't guarantee it. Depends on what the weatherman wants."

"The weatherman? He controls the weather, not... ." Maddie shook her head. "Can I try it, then?"

"Why are you in such a hurry to leave? You said yourself, these downpours never last long. Stay 'til it's over."

"It's Jim. He'll be mad at me. I'm always late and today I promised him I'd be home on time." She turned back to the old crone, pleading with her eyes. "Let me try."

The old crone shook her head. "It would be better for you to stay here. It's safe here."

"Yes, but Jim..."

"...Can wait a little longer."

Maddie leant up against the locked door and closed her eyes. The old crone was right really. It was warm here, and dry, and there really was no guarantee the blanket would keep her safe against the onslaught. And really, what could Jim do if she was late again? Surely he would understand. She knew he would not.

She sighed and opened her eyes to the compassionate, all-seeing eyes of the old woman.

"I have to go to Jim." She resigned herself to the barrage she knew would come when she walked in the door.

The old woman nodded, hiding the sorrow in her eyes.

Maddie wrapped the blanket tightly around her and stepped out into the rain once more. She turned back to wave farewell to the old woman, but she was no longer there.

***

At first light the rain stopped and the city looked sparkling and clean. Once again people ventured out and the city teemed with life.

Jim yawned and stretched as he rolled out of bed. The house was silent, unnaturally so. Maddie had never been this late before and he had fallen asleep before she came in.

"She'll be sleeping on the sofa," he thought, and made his way into the front room. There was no sign of her, but he wasn't worried as he thought perhaps she had opted to spend the night with a friend. He thought she would have called, though, but the power was out last night so it may not have been possible.

He switched on the television to the news, just in time to see the weatherman promise another dry, sultry day with the chance of a shower in the evening.

"Don't get caught out without your umbrella!" he said. Jim's gaze was drawn to the umbrella stand by the front door. Maddie's acid-proof umbrella still stood there. He couldn't believe she had forgotten it.

The doorbell chimed and his heart lurched.

"Maddie! Did you forget your keys, too!" he said, and flung the door wide.

An old crone with beady eyes stood there. She clasped a battered hold-all in her bird-like grip.

"Does this belong here?" She handed Jim the hold-all, compassion warming her beady eyes a little as she watched Jim's face drain of all colour. It was Maddie's. He trembled, fighting tears and panic as he tenderly took the hold-all from the old woman's grasp.

"No one takes the weatherman's warning seriously." The old woman turned away and vanished. Jim didn't notice.

"I told her not to be late," he whispered.

Point of View: It's all relative, really

STEPS TO HEAVEN

One, and two, and three, and four, and five... Joel climbs the steps leading to his holiday let in East Looe.

And six, and seven, and eight, and nine, and ten... His shopping is beginning to weigh heavily – just a couple of things: a loaf of bread, some ham and cheese, butter, jar of coffee, sugar – basics to help make his stay a little more comfortable. It's not a lot, but the climb along the steeply winding paths from the Co-op to the bottom of the steps that would take him further aloft to his accommodation perched somewhere on the hill above the seaside town has left him winded. He is considerably better after his long stay in hospital, from which he had chosen to convalesce in Looe, but he is still 'a tad' unfit.

Eleven, and twelve, thirteen, fourteen, fifteen, sixteen ...

"Good morning." A woman he recognises as staying in the house next to his passes him on the steps. She is dressed in a pale pink padded coat which make her legs clad in caramel leggings appear spindly. He thinks she looks a little like a Popsicle. A bobble hat holds most of her blonde wind-whipped hair in place and a small rucksack, which is casually flung over her shoulder, catches a bit more. The rest flies about her head in a frenzy, whipping her face ... and his, too, as she passes him on the steps.

She catches his eye and grins, a little self-consciously, as they pass each other.

"You off to the shops, then?" he asks, more to be polite than for any real desire to chat.

"Ahh, yeah," she replies and stops to engage the handsome stranger in some banal conversation about the particularly cold spell they are experiencing.

"Not at all like last year, is it?" she says. "Don't you think the sun shining on the sea makes it look almost Mediterranean, all blue, and deliciously inviting, but frigidly deceptive? Many times this month ({and remember it's been so cold it's snowed, but not here in Looe – too much salt in the air, chases the snow away, don't you know), anyway, I've been so tempted to take the plunge, but d'you remember the young man who dived in to retrieve his girlfriend's watch this time last year when it wasn't as cold? Anyway, he wasn't in for too long but still had to be rushed to Derriford – hypothermia, you understand."

Joel cuts into her rhetoric, anxious now to get to

the top of the stairs and the relative safety of his temporary home, and somehow he convinces her to carry on down the steps. He watches until she turns the corner at the bottom. Then he turns away, takes a deep breath and resumes his climb.

Fourteen, fifteen... no. Where was I? Twelve... no!

He looks back down, tries to re-count the steps he's already climbed but can't be sure he hasn't counted that one already.

"Oh, dammit!" he exclaims, and with a resigned sigh he retraces his steps, "Sixteen! It was sixteen." Once at the bottom, he looks up again at the mountain of steps.

"What kind of fool builds a town all over such a steep hill?!" he grumbles to himself. "And what kind of fool decides to recuperate in said place?"

One, and two, and three, and four, and five – quicker so as to make it up there.

And six, and seven, and eight, and nine, and ten, eleven, and twelve, thirteen, fourteen, fifteen – all in strict marching rhythm, helps him to concentrate.

Lifting his right foot, placing it on the step and shifting his weight to his right foot; lifting his left foot, bringing it up and forward to the next step, counting as he climbs, deliberately, in time.

Sixteen, seventeen, eighteen, slower now, the burn just beginning.

"Keep going!" Puffed, he breathes the words.

Nineteen, twenty, counting all the way.

Twenty-one, twenty-two, twenty-three, twenty-four, twenty-five ...

He hears the kids before he sees them and keeps his head down, refusing to make eye contact, counting his way up the steps, mouthing the words... *twenty-six, twenty-seven, twenty-eight...*

"You're a bit young to be loopy, aint ya mista?" a mocking voice taunts him. He's still a few steps away and Joel looks up, seeing a precocious, spotty teenager wearing black skinny jeans, his head hidden by a black hoodie.

Twenty-nine, thirty, thirty-one....

"Hey! Wotcha counting for? My ma used to count if I were in trouble."

"Yeah, mine, too," the spotty teenager's equally spotty friend rebutted. "Think she could only count to three, though."

Raucous laughter follows and the other lads with them plonk down the steps, ever closer.

Thirty-two, thirty-three (I hope they just keep walking), thirty-... oh dammit. He had kept climbing, forgetting to count and now has lost his place. He groans, frustrated, resigned.

"You must have been a good kid if you're mum only had to count three." His rejoinder surprises the lads. They stop. They're not sure if he's joking, mocking, or deadly serious. Either way, they have no idea what he's talking about. He sighs and stops, too.

"Wha...?" Unison.

"Well, when my mum started counting, it meant I was in trouble. She very rarely stopped at three..."

"Well, yeah. We all had that..." their spokesman appears to be the pimply one. He postures, a little uncertainly.

Joel sighs again. "I doubt it." His shoulders droop and he remembers. He mentally shakes himself and resumes his climb.

Where was I this time? The lads are bored with him and continue to lope down the stairs, leaping two or three at a time, whooping it up. Joel stands still until they have gone. He's nearly in tears. He's forgotten where he is up to and knows he has to start again. He turns around and looks back down the steps, then up and realises that he's almost half-way. He makes a decision and leaves his shopping on the step and runs down to the bottom as fast as he dares, clinging to the handrail. At the bottom, he stops to collect his breath and his thoughts, to clear his mind.

"I'm gonna do it this time – no-one and nothing can distract me."

He takes a deep breath and for the third time this morning, he begins to count.

One, and two, and three, and four, and five, and six, and seven, and eight, and nine, and ten, eleven, and twelve, thirteen, fourteen, fifteen, sixteen, seventeen, eighteen, nineteen, twenty…

He's off to a good start, and stops to catch his breath and gather his strength, repeating 'twenty' over and over in his head. Calmer now, he continues…

Twenty-one, twenty-two, twenty-three, twenty-four, twenty-five, twenty-six, twenty-seven, twenty-eight, twenty-nine, thirty…

He plods along, slow and steady, ever upwards, closer to the top.

Thirty-one, thirty-two, thirty-three, thirty-four, thirty-five, thirty-six, thirty-seven, thirty-eight, thirty-nine, forty…

His laboured breath rings in his ears and his heart pounds strongly in his head. Still, he forces himself on.

Forty-one, forty-two, forty-three, forty-four, forty-five, forty-six, forty-seven, forty-eight, forty-nine, fifty, fifty-one, fifty-two, fifty-three, fifty-four, fifty-five, fifty-six, fifty-seven, fifty-eight, fifty-nine, sixty…

He mentally blocks everything else out, his pounding head, raw, gasping breath, aching legs… He unzips his coat and the rush of cool air is momentarily refreshing.

Sixty-one, sixty-two, sixty-three, sixty-four, sixty-five, sixty-six, sixty-seven, sixty-eight, sixty-nine, seventy, seventy-one, seventy-two, seventy-three, seventy-four, seventy-five, seventy-six, seventy-seven, seventy-eight, seventy-nine...

He's like a robot now, plodding ever upward, slowly. He stops, looks up and is surprised to find he's almost there. The realisation fills him with the courage to keep going.

Eighty, eighty-one, eighty-two, eighty-three, eighty-four, eighty-five, eighty-six!

He's made it up the steps and stumbles to the bench someone in another lifetime has kindly put there. His face glows fiery furnace red and his aching limbs match the burn. He lowers his frame onto the seat, inhales deeply and exhales slowly, several times, feeling the oxygen slowly returning to replenish his soul. Gradually his temperature cools and his body begins to tingle. His sweat dries and he begins to itch. He still has a little way to go up the hill to the house, but the steps are the worse.

Feeling a little lightheaded after the exercise, he stands to survey his success. The view from the top of the steps is magnificent; the boats bob gently in the harbour and the winter sun bounces off the ripples, causing momentary blindness. His eyes adjust and he lowers his gaze to the mountain of steps he has just climbed.

He cannot believe how far away the bottom step is, and he is proud of his accomplishment.

"Eighty-six steps! Man, I'm a god!"

His eyes clear fully and he notices something on a step a little over half-way down and he feels his stomach drop. Frantically he looks around him, at the bench, at the top of the steps, at the path in between. His shopping bag is not near.

"Oh my …" He wants to scream, but something inside won't let him. He has to be in control. He has to…

"Oh, dammit!"

Joel approaches the steps, resigned. He won't be going home any time soon.

One, and two, and three, and four…

SECRETS

Annabelle sat on a pile of cushions, bathed in moonlight, soothing jazz on the stereo. Soon she'd do something about the mess, when she has found the energy.

JJ finally slept. He was teething, and even had an ear infection. A baby in pain! Not pleasant. However, the day was over and she could relax.

It was nearly midnight and her growling stomach reminded her of her hunger. Jack would be home soon.

"He'll want to eat when he comes in," she sighed.

***

The old man is heavy on her. She can hardly breathe. His sour breath overwhelms her. Rancid sweat drips onto her flesh as he satisfies his lust with her nine-year-old body. She shudders.

"Do you like this, honey," misinterpreting her shudder of disgust.

She squeezes her eyes shut and silently prays.

She hurts, but it's no use crying out. There's no one to rescue her.

Someone knocks at the caravan door.

"Joe, you there?"

"I'm busy," he growls. The would-be visitor leaves and Joe rolls off.

"He spoiled it."

She gulps in a huge breath and regrets it. His rank body odour and sour breath rush into her lungs. She fights the urge to vomit, and lies there, shivering.

"Get dressed and git!" he orders her.

***

With a weary sigh, Annabelle started preparing dinner. It was too late for anything exotic. She marinated the steak, tossed a salad and put some wine on ice. Then she set the table, adding a small floral arrangement. A candle completed the picture. She lit the candle, and stepped back to survey her work.

"Nice," she said. "I'll cook the steak when he gets in." She blew out the candle.

Annabelle had a quick shower, applied a bit of make-up and dressed in the outfit Jack liked best. The red dress hugged her slim figure, and she piled her long, black hair loosely on her head with wispy tendrils snaking around her face and slender neck. The result was a soft, alluring look. She relit the candle and sat down to wait.

At 12.30, when she had just about given him up, she heard the key turn in the lock.

***

She no longer lives in the caravan park, and the old man is probably dead by now. Grandma is out for the day, and now that she's done her homework, she relaxes with a bit of jazz. She settles comfortably on the sofa, her head resting on a cushion.

It's her final year at secondary school. She studies hard, and hopes it'll be good enough.

The key turns in the lock.

"Hey, Grandma, did you forget something!"

"Hi, there, Little Red Riding Hood! Come show me your basket of goodies, and I'll show you mine."

She opens her eyes and sees her dead father's older brother, leering at her.

"What do you want?" she says. She already knows.

"Come on. You know you like it," and he kneels down beside her, caressing her, preparing her for the onslaught.

She learnt long ago that to refuse him, meant pain for her. But if she closes her eyes, her mind will take her miles away, to her secret place, a place of healing.

He finishes, zips himself up and throws her clothes at her.

"Better get dressed. We don't want your Grandmother to find out what a slut you really are." He leaves, locking the door behind him.

She stands under the shower, washing away the guilt, the dirt, the shame. Her body is clean, but the taint remains.

***

Jack stumbled into the flat, tripping over the mat.

"What the …" he mumbled. "Where's the lights?"

"Belle!" he hollered.

Oh, God, he's drunk.

"Hey, Honey, you hungry? Dinner's almost done. You've time for a quick shower if you like."

He ignored her, heading for the wine.

"Not a bad drop."

She lit the stove, trying to stop shaking. It wasn't the first time he'd come home like this, and it probably wouldn't be the last.

Jack popped the cork and, ignoring the glasses, took a hearty swig straight from the bottle.

"Place is a mess. What you been doing all day?"

"JJ's been sick…"

"You use that kid as an excuse for everything. Too

busy preening, no doubt. Waste of money, that gumph! Makes you look ugly. Ughh." He took another swig of the bottle, and returned it to the ice bucket.

Silently, she cooked the steak, arranged it neatly on the two plates with the salad.

"Haven't you eaten?" Belligerent.

"I didn't get a chance," she said quietly, and poured herself a glass of wine.

Jack snatched the bottle from her.

She picked at her meal, suddenly not very hungry, and when he'd finished, she stood and cleared the dishes. She turned towards the bedroom.

"Where're you going?" he yelled.

"Oh, for Pete's sake, keep your voice down. JJ's only been asleep about an hour. I'm tired. I'm going to bed. Coming?"

"You ordering me around? When you bring money into this house instead of ... whatever it is you do..., then ... just maybe, you can tell me what to do. In the meantime, keep your trap shut."

JJ started crying, and with a resigned sigh, Annabelle went to him. Jack stormed after her.

"Leave the bloody kid cry!"

She ignored him and opened the door to JJ's bedroom.

"I told you to come here," Jack snarled, crossing the remaining distance with one stride and striking her across the back of her head.

She stopped, momentarily stunned, then turned to face him.

"Jack," she pleaded, "JJ's sick. I just need to settle him first, then..."

"I said, come here." Menacing.

It was dangerous to cross him, but her baby was crying.

"I'll be there in a minute." Softly. Resigned.

Here we go again, she thought.

***

She's having so much fun at the party. With her degree completed she can relax. Music empowers her; she's in control, calling the shots.

Mick invites her outside to cool off. She goes.

It's a perfect night for lovers, starlit and crisp, though a little chilly. She shivers.

"Cold?"

She nods. He drapes his jacket around her shoulders.

It's getting colder and she'd really like to go in now. He says not yet.

He moves closer and kisses her. It feels nice. She kisses him back. His lips arouse pleasant feelings. She responds ardently and his kisses become more urgent. Before she knows it, she's on the ground.

"Mick, stop." He doesn't listen.

"I know you want it, Baby."

She sobs.

Finally he's through.

"That was great!" He helps her to her feet.

Back in the dance hall she leaves him and heads towards the Ladies. One of Mick's friends grabs her roughly by her arm.

"Hey, Baby. My turn."

***

Annabelle regained consciousness to find Jack snoring beside her in their bed. JJ was sniffling in the other room. Her body ached and her head was pounding.

JJ had cried himself into a semi-sleep, but when Annabelle touched his shaking shoulders, he flinched, and woke with a start.

"Shhh, Mummy's here." She held him close, pacing the length of the lounge room.

The warmth of his little body soothed her, and when he finally went to sleep, she gently laid him on the couch beside her. She sat, thinking for a while, and when her mind could take no more in, she fell into an exhausted sleep.

***

Six weeks after the party and she's pregnant.

Jack, the last one to take her outside, has called every day since. He says he loves her. She gives him a call.

"Can I see you?"

"I'll be right over," and in ten minutes, he's there.

She looks beautiful but pale. He kisses her passionately. His passion turns to urgency. It's no use resisting; besides, it'll soften him up.

"Jack," her head rests on his chest, "I'm pregnant."

Jack is speechless. His heart misses a beat, then thumps harder and stronger. Finally, he speaks.

"We'll get married, a quiet wedding. As soon as possible."

This is what she was secretly hoping for.

They're married a month later.

***

It was morning. Jack was in the shower. Her neck ached; her whole body ached. JJ still slept, his cheeks no longer feverish. Annabelle breathed a sigh of relief. Today would be better.

She washed last night's dishes and prepared Jack's breakfast. A full English as she always did after an exceptionally bad night.

"Love you, Babe," he purred, ignoring her bruised face and throat.

"I know," she said, lightly.

Jack finished his breakfast.

"I'll be late, again," he said. "Mick's birthday. I'm eating there."

He kissed her bruised lips – too hard – and left.

It was quiet. She had a quick shower while JJ slept. Annabelle grimaced when she saw herself in the mirror. Make-up helped a little to restore her face, and a light scarf covered the bruises on her neck. Sunglasses would hide her eyes.

With the house tidied and their meagre possessions packed into a couple of suitcases, Annabelle made some calls and wrote a note to Jack. A short half-hour later a taxi picked them up. Hours later they reached their destination.

"We're here, Sweetie," she whispered softly to JJ as the taxi pulled into the driveway. She paid the driver and unloaded her luggage into the little cottage by the sea.

***

It's after midnight. The flat is dark. Jack turns the key in the lock, carefully, so as not to wake her. He switches on the lamp.

The pristine tidiness is marred by the crisp white envelope on the mantle.

"Jack," he reads, "I can't take this any more. I deserve better than this. Please don't try to find us."

Numbly, he lowers his handsome frame onto the couch. They've gone.

***

It's a small place, but safe and warm. Firelight dances on stone walls and the comforting shadows are the ghosts of her parents. She's lived here before, in happier days.

Annabelle breathes deeply, picks up a sleepy JJ and heads outside. A fresh breeze whips her. She holds JJ up to the sky. He gurgles with delight as she spins him around. Then she gathers him close and runs with the wind in her hair and the sweet song of love in her heart.

.

JOHNNY-B-GOODE

I used to laugh every time I watched the old *Lost in Space* re-runs my parents watched when they were my age. They were so lame! Mum said she always knew the robot was there to protect Will so she wasn't scared. Dad was a different story. I thought he must have been a coward. Chicken. Lily-livered. Jumping at shadows. But then it happened, and I knew there was a lot out there to be frightened of. I only wish I had a robot to protect me. Perhaps if I had, I wouldn't have a story to tell now. But then again...

The day began ordinarily enough when my alarm blared out Good Charlotte's *The Anthem*. I groaned and rolled over, squeezing my eyes shut, forcing my mind to return to my dream-date, the gorgeous Jordana in the grade six class next to mine. Yeah, I know. I'm really too young to date, but you're never too young to dream, right? It was no use. She was gone and I knew she wasn't coming back.

Mum pounded on my door.

"Johnny! Get a move on! You'll be late!" she called as she passed my door on her way to wake up the twins. I groaned again, mumbled something I knew she wouldn't hear and dragged myself out of bed. By the time I had pulled on my uniform and shoved my books into my bag, the twins were preening in the bathroom, and I had to wait again.

"Hurry up!" I growled at them. I knew if I didn't get into the bathroom soon, I'd never get a chance. Mum would make me do the lunches and set the table, and the girls would get out of doing their jobs again. Life is really unfair when you're the oldest and you have irritating twins for sisters.

Still, today I had my chance in the bathroom and the girls made the lunches. Their secret giggles and whispers should have warned me, but I just thought they were doing things year fours do all the time. Big seventh graders ignore such things, but today I really shouldn't have.

I know I'm dribbling like my baby brother when Mum tries to feed him, but I guess I don't really know how to get it all out. I think I just have to tell you about my day, and then maybe you'll understand. And maybe you won't think I'm all bad. At least, that's what I hope.

I choked down a couple of vegemite toasts washed down by some milk, wiped my face on the back of my hand and ran out the door. Mum, of course, called me back and told me to walk with my sisters, and, still being a kid and a bit scared of her, I had to do what she said. Hey, you better not tell anyone else I'm still a bit scared of my Mum! To tell the truth, I'm not really scared of her. I just respect her too much to not do what I'm told. OK?

Well, I walked to school with the twin monsters, and just as we got to the gate, it all started.

The lollypop lady takes her dog everywhere with her. Molly's real old, and I guess she doesn't like to be left at home alone. Actually, the lollypop lady's pretty wrinkly, too. Anyway, we waited behind the yellow line just like we're s'posed to and when the old bag blew her whistle we crossed the road. Nothing unusual there, but ... when we got close to the old lady's dog, the poor thing just went nuts. I mean, she barked and barked, and yelped like she was in pain and kept trying to bite the end of her tail. Then she'd scratch her ears, do a little whine, and bark and yelp some more.

"Hey, Johnny, whatcha do to Mrs Stevens' dog?" Penny, the oldest twin monster yelled.

"Nuthin'," I hissed back at her. "Shuddup would ya!"

I went to walk through the gate, but now the stupid dog barred my way. I couldn't believe it was the same dog, her fangs looked monstrous and dripped with foaming spit. She growled deep in her throat and I swear her eyes turned red and all glowing like. I didn't like this one bit, so I turned away. I was going to go to the other gate, but as soon as I turned my back, the dog leaped at me.

I didn't see it coming. Her sharp claws scraped my shoulder, ripping my bag and dragging me backwards. I almost fell, and if I had, I just know I'd be dog food by now. Somehow I found the strength to pull away and ran off to a safe distance. Molly was always on a chain, and I think that's what saved me this time.

Gabby, the other twin monster stared at me.

"You musta done something to get her mad like that!" she exclaimed. "She's so old she wouldn't hurt a flea. Whatcha do, Johnno?"

I just glared at her and then walked away. I hadn't gone far when I heard the crowd around the school gate gasp. I didn't want to look back, but I knew I had to, if just because I was so curious. There was Molly, straining at her chain, growling her horrifying growls, her shiny red eyes fixed on me. Her neck had veins that popped out, just like Arnold Schwarznegger's muscles and I could swear I saw a grin on her face. She licked her lips with that long, slimy tongue, and I shuddered.

And there was the chain, stretching and getting longer. The more she stretched, the closer she got to me, and the closer she got to me, the thinner that chain got. I knew I had to move. I had to run to get away from there before that chain snapped. It wouldn't be long, I just knew it, but the more I tried to move, the harder it was. I felt like I was a concrete statue - living and breathing, but unable to move my legs.

I wondered what old Mrs Stevens was doing. Couldn't she see her dog was trying to maul me? I had to look, but I was afraid to take my eyes off that mad dog. Just a little peek, then, and oh, boy, do I wish I hadn't.

Mrs Stevens didn't look like Mrs Stevens any more. She was taller somehow, and a lot less wrinkled, as if she was stretching to her real height and the wrinkles were just a disguise. I stood with my mouth open - catching flies, my dad would call it. She looked terrible, and the hungry look on her face was just like the look on Molly's. They were both hungry, and they both wanted to EAT ME! What could I do? Just about the whole school was there, by now, to see what all the fuss was, and those closest to it all were frozen solid. Well, actually, I'm sure they were still alive, but they weren't moving, just like me.

I was terrified, and to my mind came the robot's warning: "Danger, Will Robinson!"

"Oh for the love of Pete!" I shouted, "what is **with** you people!"

Nobody said a word and it seemed to me then as if they were waiting to see what would happen, and I don't think I liked the weird looks that came over them when Molly's chain stretched so thin you could see the colour of the concrete through it. The onlookers looked just as hungry as old Mrs Stevens and her dog Molly.

Suddenly the chain snapped - not with a loud crack like I was expecting but with a musical tinkle, like the time I dropped Mum's favourite crystal vase and it shattered on the tiles. Immediately, my legs thawed and I ran. I didn't know where I was running to, or what I was going to do when I got there. I only knew I had to give myself a fighting chance, and staying here to get chewed out by Mrs Stevens, her rabid dog and a pack of ravenous classmates was not going to help.

I ran down the footpath, passed the preschool and round the corner. My breath echoed in my head, and a sharp pain stabbed at my side.

"Great!" I muttered. "What a time to get a stitch!"

I had to keep going so I did. I ran the whole school block, sped by the school dentist and darted across the road. The guy at the post office looked at me real weird, as did the lady who always gave us extra chips at the takeaways. Even the ladies getting their hair done at the salon, and the pretty hairdresser looked at me. I hoped they didn't look like the kids at school. If they were going to chase me too, I was in real trouble.

By now I was literally gasping for breath, but I knew if I stopped, I was a goner. I came to the beach steps, and flew down them, skidding to get direction at the bottom. Behind me I could hear the raspy breath of Molly, and the pounding of hundreds of school shoes as my chasers relentlessly followed.

Boy was I unfit! But it's surprising how fit you are when you're life depends on it! I did not want to become dog food - or people food for that matter. This was getting grosser, the more I thought about it.

"Don't think. Don't think," I told myself over and over again. "Run! Run! Run!"

And so run I did, along the waterfront, down to the jetty, past the lagoon and on to Sommer's Beach. I was getting real tired, but I didn't dare stop. Then it dawned on me – go home! I don't know why I didn't think of it sooner. Mum was at work, but I had a key, and my balmy sisters didn't. I could lock myself in, and when Mum came home, she would save me. Yes! It was a brilliant plan.

I made an abrupt right turn up Sunshine Street, heading back to Brampton Ave. It was only a small hill, but oh boy, did I feel it. I had been on the go now for maybe an hour. Have you ever tried running for so long? I was dead. Actually, I wished I was.

My bag was getting heavier, and my legs felt like when you've been swimming for a while and try to get out of the pool in the deep end. I was wasted! Still I had to keep going. I looked behind me and they were still coming. Not as fast now, but still gaining on me. I ran down towards the Ambulance and thought about running inside, but I was nearly home now. Besides, I couldn't lock myself inside the ambulance office, now, could I?

Just a few more streets and I would be home.

"I just can't run anymore!" I managed to cry out between my tortured gasps. I looked up and realised I had made it home. Look, I'm a grown boy, but I have to admit it – I cried with relief when I saw my house.

I threw down my bag and ripped open the zip. Aah! My keys! I grabbed my open bag, and spilling the contents all over the lawn, I ran up the stairs. Actually, I stumbled up the stairs, I was just so tired. Fumbling with the key in the lock, I could hear the mob coming closer. I was shaking so much I nearly dropped the key, but finally, I was inside. I slammed the door shut, locked it and fell back against it. Safe at last!

My chest heaved as I gulped in the safe air of home. Outside, the noise of the mob was fainter. Carefully, I turned around and peeked through the curtains. Some of them were rummaging through the contents of my bag. Others looked like they were sniffing to find something. Mrs Stevens and Molly were clumping up the stairs. Molly's tongue lolled to the side and I could see she was having trouble breathing. Mrs Stevens, on the other hand, looked younger than I'd ever seen her – as if the exercise had actually done her some good. They both still looked extremely hungry.

"Danger! Will Robinson!" There was that voice again, echoing in my empty head.

I shrank back from the window and dragged Mum's doll cabinet to the door, pushing it up tight against the doorknob. The door was locked, I know, but those two looked as if they could walk through doors. Hopefully the doll cabinet would stop them.

The noise on the front lawn had now stopped, and I couldn't hear Mrs Stevens or Molly on the stairs. I was terrified, but just had to look. Through the curtain, I saw an amazing sight. My twin sisters were holding their tummies, they were laughing so hard. Someone held up my lunch box in triumph and threw it to the amazingly young-looking Mrs Stevens. Molly sat on her back legs wagging her tail and with the grin on her face all dogs have when they're waiting for something delicious.

Mrs Stevens opened my lunch box, and to my amazement brought out what looked like my sandwich Penny had made this morning. It was crawling with all sorts of things. I couldn't tell what they were, but they were making the most horrid clicking and whirring sounds imaginable. The mob on the lawn bowed to the ground as if to some sort of God.

Suddenly, a blue glow came from the things on my sandwich. My sisters stopped in mid-giggle and stared at the things in horror. The clicking metal insect things – well, that's what they looked like to me – began to move together, and incredible as it sounds, they joined together until a mini robot rested in Mrs Stevens' hand. She held it high for all the mob to see and they cheered. Even my sisters seemed to be cheering – or they could have been screaming, I couldn't really tell.

The cheering got louder and louder, and the louder they got, the bigger the little robot grew. In no time at all, it was as big as Mrs Stevens before she grew taller and lost her wrinkles. The robot chirped a bit like R2D2 of Star Wars and then it turned around and faced the door. I gasped. Surely the door lock was no match for a robot.

Horrible scratching noises came from the other side of the door. Somehow I knew that doll cabinet was not going to stop it. Mum would kill me if anything happened to her precious dolls, but I couldn't move it back now. I backed myself up until I was against the wall and squeezed my eyes shut. Perhaps if I didn't look, it would all go away.

No such luck. The scraping, scratching and chirping noises grew louder and louder. Outside on the lawn, the mob began chanting something I couldn't make out. I strained to hear. I was getting a headache. All that extra exercise this morning was catching up with me. I was aching all over. Still, I kept my eyes shut and willed it all to go away.

Suddenly there was a crash! My eyes flew open and I immediately wished they hadn't. The robot was in my house! Mum's dolls were in pieces on the floor and I just knew I was in for it now. I had no energy left to run. I had nowhere else to run to. I let out a sob as the robot reached out to me. It shook my arm, gently at first, but then it got harder and harder. I tried to pull free, but it was no use. The harder I pulled, the harder it shook.

"Johnny!"

It knew my name. I screamed in terror!

"Johnny!"

It was calling me again. I flung my other arm up over my head.

"Leave me alone!" I screamed.

"Johnny! It's me! Mum!"

Slowly I opened my eyes. Mum was kneeling beside my bed. How the hell did I get here? I was so confused.

"Where's the robot?" I asked.

"Robot? What robot?" asked Mum. "Look, Johnny, I told you half an hour ago to get up for school. You'll have to go to bed earlier, and stop watching those *Lost in Space* re-runs. You know they give you nightmares!"

I sat up and rubbed my eyes. I could hear my twin sisters preening in the bathroom.

"The girls have made your lunch for you," said Mum. "Now hurry up, get dressed and eat your breakfast."

I stuffed myself into my uniform, crammed my books into my bag and threw in my lunch box. Stuffing two pieces of vegemite toast down my throat, I washed them down a glass of milk and wiped my face with the back of my hand. I was ready.

"Come on, Twin Monsters!" I called as I left the

house.

Thank goodness it was only a dream! I walked to school with the twins, crossed the road when Mrs Stevens told us to and patted Molly as I walked past.

And as I walked past, Molly began to bark and whine and yelp and try to bite her tail and scratch at her ears.............

PHOTOGRAPHIC MEMORY

Like Dorian Gray and his painting, I just knew that if I even glanced at the photograph, all the happy memories we had ever shared would vanish, and I'd be left to my misery, or to die, whichever punishment was deemed to be the worst.

I took a deep breath, squared my shoulders, said a silent prayer for strength and entered the room. Someone was playing soft music on the baby grand and the quiet hum of subdued conversation sounded loud to my over-sensitive ears. I tried to ignore the incessant buzzing in my head which was threatening to overtake me completely. I focussed on the seat I chose, making a bee-line for it, not intending to stop for anyone or anything.

I had nearly made it when someone called my name. I groaned inwardly, summoned my strength and lifted my head to acknowledge the speaker. Pete, a jolly rotund friend, enveloped me in his customary bear hug, crushing my body to his. His hug had forced my head up, level with the photograph and I squeezed my eyes shut, shuddering at the nearness of my escape.

"How are you holding up?" he murmured, gently stroking my tense shoulders.

It was an intimately platonic gesture, and usually his hugs were just what I needed. Today I just didn't want to be touched. I needed to be alone in the crowd I knew would gather. I murmured some meaningless response and extricated myself from his grasp.

I averted my eyes as I passed the stand where I knew the photograph had been placed, but it was impossible to avoid it altogether. I had almost made it before I thought I detected a movement out of the corner of my eye, and narrowly avoided being turned to stone, or worse, being consigned to eternal misery as I fought the urge to turn and gaze on such beauty. Of all the photographs we had ever taken of her, why did he have to choose this one?

I closed my eyes. Memories of that day came flooding back, threatening to open another floodgate I have firmly closed against such an occurrence. So far it was working, but the painful lump in my throat told me the deluge was threatening. And I knew it wouldn't take too much to release the torrent.

***

Sara stood on the platform, poised to make the

dive that would give her the national championship. Well, not really. We were just having a bit of fun in the local pool and the 'diving platform' was merely one of the starter blocks at the deep end.

"Watch me!" she shouted, and, like I had so many times before, I did. She was so graceful as she bent to take the dive, toes curled over the edge, hands hanging loosely by them, gently swinging. Then she stood up.

"Pretend I'm in a race!" she squealed. "You tell me when to go."

I indulged her.

"Ready!" I yelled, and she returned to her starting position, toes curled, arms like a rag doll's.

"Steady!" A little slower, building the tension. I paused for effect, and was rewarded with Sara's blue eyes peeking at me from her curtain of soggy ash-blond hair. I grinned at her.

"GO!" I shouted.

Sara flung herself forward with all the gusto of an Olympic swimmer, her body flying through the air for a few seconds before cutting a neat swathe in the water, slicing down, her legs together until the last moment when she lost control and they flopped in to the water to create an inelegant splash. If only she had the style of an Olympic swimmer, I remember thinking. Still, her *joie de vivre* was her style and it was infectious.

I watched as she swam the length of that pool so many times that day. I had to cajole her to stop for food, drink, to put on her sun block, and she never showed signs of slowing down or tiring. I grew tired just watching her boundless energy. If she wasn't racing imaginary competitors, she was swimming around in a make-believe water kingdom where she was the mermaid princess.

I'm not sure what role I played in all this, but I do remember taking a few snaps, capturing the princess to immortalise her as she was. I didn't know that was what I was doing. I thought I was just providing her with scrapbook fodder, something to show the kids in days to come, a long way off in the future.

When the sun finally began to set and the lifeguards had blown their last whistle, Sara conceded that she was really just a human earth child after all, and the water fantasies of the day melded into reality. She showered the chlorine off her skin, dried herself and dressed in her flowery sundress, even though the sun had now long gone to sleep and the coolness of the evening descended. Still she wanted more. Did her energy not have bounds? I was beginning to despair of ever finding my bed that night.

"Let's go to the flicks," she suggested.

"You're not tired?" I asked, stifling a yawn and trying to stretch muscles aching from disuse.

"Nah."

"Hungry?"

"A little, maybe."

"How about a Subway sandwich then, and maybe a video when we get home."

She was disappointed, I could tell, but I just couldn't face another couple of hours sitting somewhere that wasn't home. She must have known because she conceded and we ate our Subway sandwiches, drank our juice, nibbled our deliciously warm and fragrant Mrs Field's cookies that simply melted in our mouths and made our way back to the car.

I wish now we'd gone on to the movies.

I can honestly say I didn't see it coming. One minute we were crossing the road, seconds from where I'd parked the car, and the next minute, I was flat on my back in the middle of the street.

Sara was nowhere to be found – at least, from my lack of vantage point, I couldn't see her.

"Sara!" I screamed, but the only sound to escape my tight throat was a hoarse whisper.

From out of a misty dream, I could hear voices.

"I didn't see them. Honest." A male voice, thick with something I couldn't identify – emotion, drink, fatigue, or pain – pleaded with someone to understand.

My head was still taken over by a swarm of bees. The incessant humming was driving me insane, but all I could see was the twinkling lights on inky blackness of the city night sky. Distant sirens advancing drove the bees from my brain. The numbness was wearing off and I was beginning to feel the pain.

An ambulance pulled up at the end of the street and I felt, rather than saw, the frenzied control the paramedics operated under. Two men fussed over me and I tried to communicate my need for them to find Sara. I must have seemed like a mad woman. They ignored my wishes, concentrating instead on me.

"Sara!" I whispered again, and this time, the younger of the two attending me peered into my face.

"She said something, sounded like 'Sara'."

"Could be the dead girl's name." The dispassionate delivery was almost too much. If I'd have had more control over my body I would have screamed and clawed at him for having dared to say such a thing, even in jest. They couldn't have been talking about my Sara. She was very much alive. I would have known if she was dead. The sudden sharp pain in my arm was in stark contrast to the dull ache in my heart. And then blissful darkness. I remembered no more.

***

"She's coming round." The voice was coming from a tunnel and as I slowly opened my eyes, the room around me gradually sharpened, coming into focus. It was a sickly green colour lit by the unnatural fluorescent light. An incessant pinging sound vied for prominence and the muted sounds of people scurrying outside the room was like a sound flood. I was disoriented at first, but then vivid memories flooded my mind and I think I cried out.

"Shhh! His soothing tones should have quieted my nerves but I was tightly sprung and thrashed out, trying to escape.

"Sara!" I cried, and the man with the soothing tones smoothed my fevered brow.

"Who's Sara?"

"We were at Subway...," I whispered.

"What else do you remember?"

I screwed up my eyes in an effort to forget.

"Too much," I breathed, and in that moment, I knew the paramedic was right. Sara was dead.

***

Soft music playing a familiar tune brought me back. I was in the chapel, and right in front of me was the photograph. My eyes were brimming with tears and I had to blink them rapidly to focus, not on the photograph – Heaven Forbid! – but on the flowers, so bright and cheery, yet surprisingly scentless, a parody of their usefulness, an empty echo of a life wasted.

The preacher spoke some kind words I really don't remember, and a young lass sang a song.

Amazing Grace it was, and oh, how sweet the sound.

It was during the song when I found my gaze being drawn to the photograph. I fought it for as long as I could, but the unsaved wretch that I am could not possibly prevail against such sentiments. And so, with clenched fists tightly held by my side, I lifted my eyes to the photograph.

Sara looked back at me, her clear blue eyes boring into mine held a glint of mischief, and I swear I saw her wink. She was draped over a giant mushroom in the middle of the pool looking back over her shoulder at me, head tilted back in laughter which was now permanently etched on her face. She was gorgeous; the sunlight captured in the photograph bounced off her wet skin and created a halo around her whole body. Sara. So full of life and loving every minute of it.

I dropped my eyes again, burned by the image of such innocent beauty, feeling again the gross misjudgement that had caused Sara's death. I felt so guilty. There were many things I could have done to prevent this. We could have stayed at home, for instance. Or gone to the movies. Or lingered over our dinner. But no. I had to rush home.

The service was nearly over. I don't remember much more of it, so engrossed was I in recriminations. But what I do remember, and this most vividly of all the memories I have of Sara's funeral, is the sudden sensation of someone or something brushing against me. I was alone in the crowd, and yet, not alone.

I heard Sara's voice, muted but musical saying: "I'm gonna miss you, Leah, but it's really okay here," and I shivered as I felt ghostly fingers caress my cheek and drape themselves across my shoulders. I felt a real embrace and unchecked, the floodgates finally opened and the virtually unstoppable torrent escaped. Great sobs wracked my body and I know everyone there pitied me. I didn't care.

With the tears, the memories gushed out too, and I was overcome with remembering all the good days we'd had. It wasn't just the pool. There were the Moors, the beach, the Barbican, the Mall – even days spent at home – hers or mine. Everywhere we went Sara brought a little piece of joy with her and gave it to me, and others, so willingly. My heart ached with each memory, and there seemed to be so very many.

Finally, I was spent. The service was over and so were my tears. I risked another glance at the photograph. She was still there, smiling at me, and it suddenly dawned on me that I hadn't been turned to stone, I hadn't died, and I hadn't aged any more than I was this morning. This wasn't going to be a Dorian Gray moment after all; instead it was a moment of healing. Sara had lived a full life and her final years had been wracked with pain and forgetfulness. And yet in her last moments she taught me a valuable lesson. Life is for living!

Sara, my grandmother, was eighty-three when she died while crossing the road. She had given me so much for which I would always be grateful. I knew she was never coming back, but now, somehow it didn't matter so much to me anymore. I had her photograph.

NO STRINGS ATTACHED

He is in the arms of another woman. The old familiar pangs of jealousy tear at my heart and I don't think I can take it much longer. But I don't want to make a scene. Not here. Not now.

They look so happy together. Much happier than I have ever seen him. There is pain in my heart now, as well as the jealousy. Perhaps, I could have done things differently. But no. I have done my best. Now is not the time for personal recriminations, nor is it the time for action.

I peer through the throng of couples dancing and think I see them again. They seem closer somehow, more intimate. My heart screams at them to stop, to remember me. I watch dumbstruck as they twirl across the dance floor. I can't feel any more pain. I feel so old.

As they draw closer to where I stand hidden

behind the artificial ferns, I see for the first time what she really is. A usurper. She has come to take my place. I don't think she knows this, but she's hurting me in the process. She is young, fresh-faced and beautiful. Her gleaming chestnut hair falls in long, graceful waves down her slender straight back. I, on the other hand, am older. Much older. My face lost its youthful glow many years ago and my former beauty is a memory. My hair, once my crowning glory, is no longer the darkly shining halo of not so long ago, though still long. Grey streaks pollute the once purely youthful colour. If I had been a man, the grey would mark me as "distinguished". As a woman, I am merely old. My back, however, can neither be described as slender nor straight.

I watch them in silence, my whole being aches with the injustice of it all. I have been replaced! I thought it would never happen to me. I believed in his love. Was it all a lie?

I can't blame her; after all, he is handsome. Men retain their looks so much longer than we do. And he is irresistible. I found him quite irresistible the first time I met him, too.

Perhaps I blame her just a little after all. Surely I could never do that to any woman. I believe I have more self-respect. Perhaps all I need do is remind her that she is a woman; that I am a woman; that all women should 'stick together'. No! Then I would have to confront her and I'm not yet prepared for that.

I watch them twirl about the floor some more.

They dance well together. They meld into one fluid being, as if to be apart would be murder. If I didn't know better, I would say they were made for each other. Looks can be deceiving. He's mine. I know it, and he knows it.

I nearly come out from behind the greenery, but something prevents me and keeps me staring. My eyes only move to follow their progress around the dance floor. I must have been too pre-occupied to notice before, but now I do. Everyone is speaking to them as they pass by. Our friends look happy for them. How could they? I take a deep breath. I take ten more deep breaths and feel myself go light-headed. Now I'm going to hyperventilate and everyone will know how I'm feeling. This won't do at all. I hold my breath for twenty counts. Ah, that's better!

My vision clears and they're still there, laughing, chatting and dancing. I can see the stars in their eyes, brilliant glowing dots of light shining for all the world to see. I wonder about my own eyes. Are they shining too? Perhaps not shining exactly. Glittering. With what? Anger? Rage? Jealousy? Yes, jealousy. And a little fear thrown in. Fear? Of course. I'm an older woman. I am closer to the end of my life than its beginning. What is to become of me now? Oh, to be young. If I were young I wouldn't be where I am now, behind the greenery, watching them so happy together, my future uncertain.

I lean my forehead against the wall beside the greenery. It is so cool, so I know without touching how hot my brow must be. All these thoughts churning through my mind are causing a headache. I must not continue this useless tirade of thought. It's doing me no good. What should I replace it with? I sigh. I am almost at the end of my tether. It's been a long day and an even longer night. Well, that's how it feels. I need to resolve this so I can go home.

I'm so tired and my feet are aching. It must be from standing around because I certainly haven't been danced off my feet. She has, though. When he needed a rest, there was someone else to take his place. Sometimes he danced with her friends and once, at the very beginning of the evening, he danced with me, but mostly they danced with each other.

In sorrow I turn away. I can bear to look no more. I will gracefully walk away and leave them to it. I turn away from the scene of torture. My eyes are now hot with unshed tears. My throat aches. My heart aches more. There are no more thoughts. I'm all thought out.

My head is down as I walk towards the bar. Someone puts an arm across my shoulders. It's Matt. He's been looking for me, but I've been here all the time. He tells me to cheer up.

"It's not the end of the world," he says. How does he know that it's not? I turn to him, ready with recriminations but I have nothing to say and the lump in my throat prevents me from trying. He tenderly caresses my face. I want to flinch at his touch but it's so gentle, so loving. With his fingers, he gently lifts my chin and drops a feather-light kiss on my lips.

"It'll be all right, you'll see." His promises seem empty. I just know everything will not be all right, but I pretend it will be. I nod and force the tears further from my heart.

Oh no! They're coming towards me now. I hoped they wouldn't see me and I could escape unnoticed. It was not to be. I see their happy smiling faces and feel a cold shiver threaten to come over me. I successfully fight it off and force a smile on my face. I give them both a kiss, hers fleeting, his a little more sincere. I murmur words of congratulations through a fog of emotion that begins to engulf me. They leave shortly after amid well wishes from their guests. I can go now.

Matt offers me his arm and engulfed in emotional fog as I am, I take it. He wisely says nothing as he escorts me to the car, leaving me to my own thoughts. Once there, though, he is all business. He opens the passenger side for me and settles me comfortably in. It's good to see the age of chivalry is not yet dead in the twenty-first century. He doesn't speak until he is sitting behind the wheel.

"Well, that went without a hitch," he says, tongue in cheek. I lean back in my seat and say nothing but my thoughts are eloquent.

It's over. Everything will be fine eventually, but it's going to take some getting used to. My time is over now. It's hard to let go. At least I know he's happy. Still, I feel empty.

It's time to cut those apron strings and let my son fly free.

FIERY ANGELS

Jo's cottage under the fig tree is the only place where I can find refuge and solace. No one else comes here now. The hubbub and bedlam of the main house are not audible and this is a place where I can relax. I've tried to make sense of what happened. I look at Jo's things and read her diary, trying to see the truth of that day in my mind, trying to make the numbness go away so I can live again.

In one hand I hold the collection of notebooks that was Jo's diary. On the wall is the last sketch she was working on. Looking from one to the other only adds to my confusion. I have read the diaries and studied Jo's many sketches numerous times over the weeks since her disappearance. But there's no sense in any of it. I now treasure those pictures and chide myself on my blindness. Why did I not know of her talent sooner? Why did I not take the time to interpret the pictures, the feelings she had, the pain she must have been feeling? I may have been able to reach her.

Now it is too late. I close my eyes and see Jo's peaceful face as a host of fiery beings carry her aloft, upward on wings of fire to God only knows where. Or why. Or how.

We moved to the country nearly three years ago to escape the city smog and noise and to provide a better life for the children. There was no smog here but the noise of the rural environment abounded. There were shops nearby, too - if you didn't mind paying the exorbitant prices they demanded in the country. You could do a decent shop in the main town, nearly an hour's drive away, and that was where we usually went. We hadn't planned to shop as often as we used to yet somehow we managed to do just that.

How naive we really were - Jeremy and I. We believed we could be totally self-sufficient, growing the fruit and vegetables and the grains we would need, and keeping a few head of cattle for milk and meat, and chickens for eggs and Sunday roasts. There was nothing wrong with the theory, but fruit trees take forever to bear, planting a vegetable garden was more hard work than we imagined (though we did persevere) and at first, the chooks ate the eggs! Our first crop of wheat was a booming success - the second a failure. We never did plant a third. We did, however, manage to provide all our milk, and through that, butter, cheese of a sort and yoghurt! Success!! The cattle for meat didn't work too well though - how could we kill the children's pets?

Yes, the children. They thoroughly enjoyed the experience at first. For so long, they were caged in their suburban back yard like the chickens in the coop. Now, they had the freedom to move, to breathe, to be. Two teachers taught at the nearest school that was only down the road, and the children would either ride their bicycles or walk. The heat bothered them too, of course, but the chance to explore over-rode their discomfort.

The school situation worried me. As with any parent, I wanted the best for my children. Would the education I valued so highly for my children be jeopardised, with only two teachers shared among seven grades? My fears turned out to be nothing more substantial than a nightmare when I saw the tremendous progress each had made. I had three attending that first year, with one leaving for high school and another joining the primary school the next year.

The farm chores did not phase them. The older girls took turns at the milking, feeding the chickens, collecting the eggs and helping in the garden. Sometimes they had to weed the wheat paddock, but only in the beginning to eradicate the thistles that grew in abundance. The younger children had no responsibility, but could help as I saw fit. Generally, the chores never lasted long, and the rest of the time was their own.

There were old sheds on the property that were

still sturdy enough for children to play in, on and around, and these provided the ready-made cubby houses they enjoy so much.

Jo particularly loved these old buildings. One was by an old Moreton Bay fig. Its gnarled and knotty trunk and branches made for excellent climbing. The tree's old branches overhung the shed's roof, creating a coolness unmatched in the main house. Yet Jo could often be found on the roof, staring into space. She never heard my approach, and it was often several minutes before I could tear her attention away from her own private thoughts. I believe the shed used to be a stable: to Jo, it was her own log cabin. It had been her dream to convert it into a miniature house with windows and a door with a real lock. She said she wanted to live in it, coming into the main house only to eat and bathe. Had the shed been big enough, she would have preferred to do those things there, too.

I know a mother should not have favourites, but if I had one, it was Jo. She looked more like me than the other children, though much prettier than I ever was. Where her brothers and sisters were all varying shades of fair, her hair was raven. She had freckled skin - a trait all my children picked up from somewhere! Her green eyes were flecked with tawny brown, and while she was by no means skinny, her body was well toned and proportionate. She was built for the country. It suited her.

Jo was good at her school work - the star pupil, her teacher would tell me. I had loved school, and also done well. I, also, had once lived in a private world of my own making. I often used to wonder how I could have married and had so many children when I valued my privacy so much. I used to worry about Jo's need for privacy, and wonder if she would choose to give it up as I had done. Yet there were many ways in which Jo and I were totally different.

She loved to sketch. I had not really taken much of an interest in her sketches, not until much later. They were beautiful in a childlike way, yet more mature than her thirteen years could portray. Where her maturity came from was a mystery. She sketched in pencil views from the roof of her cabin, both real and imaginary. The real ones were stark in their exactness and dedication to detail. The ramshackle chicken coop, the old milking bail (which we still used then), the drying up dam, the endless paddocks and hills with their waving spidery grasses and knotty gums, all took on stark beauty under the guiding light of her pencil.

The imaginary ones were mostly the same scenes, but new and vibrant, as if she had been there when they were first created. Knotty gums were young and spritely, branches and leaves waved gently in the fresh breezes and the grasses were green and springy. Beautiful unblemished animals dotted her landscapes, capering in the joy of living, the pleasure of being. Looking at them, I could feel young again. I found it hard to believe my solemn, introverted daughter hid such feeling behind her self-imposed mask.

She kept a diary. I never found that until it was too late. Could I have prevented what happened? I used to think so, but I know better now. Still, I know I will always blame myself. She relied on me, but in a very real way, I was not there for her. Yet I loved her - she was my favourite - and close as we were, she never confided in me. She preferred to write it all so eloquently in a series of little notebooks with spiral spines and speckled yellow cardboard covers. I don't think I ever kept anything from my mother, but Jo felt the need to keep her deepest feelings, joys, hurts and pains all to herself.

The diary provided me with a wealth of information about my daughter. I learned she loathed school. She found the formal structure allowed for no freedom of expression. She never felt she could express herself in creative writing and art classes. The lessons were too stilted and the topics assigned were not to her liking. Learning was fun, but Jo would rather do it her way. I had no clue she felt that way.

She was a loner. Now, that I already knew. She knew everyone at the school - though how could you not in a school with a total population of 36. But they were not all friends. We were newcomers in a tight knit community, and Jo was different from the rest. When I looked honestly, I could see that she lacked friends. She never asked me if she could go to someone else's home - or to invite someone over. Her brothers' friends nearly lived at our house after school, and her older sister was always over at Mandy's doing one thing or another. Yet Jo remained alone. I thought it was by choice, and perhaps in a way it was. I don't believe Jo saw it that way.

She loved her little cottage and valued the time she could spend there. I already knew that, too, but what she wrote about that old shed helped me to see how much it really meant to her. It was more than her refuge: it was her world. Her entire days, nights, weekends revolved around her own little cottage with the tin roof under the Moreton Bay fig. Her chores were done speedily so she could return to her niche. She slept soundly at night so she could enjoy the rooftop and sketch her world with freshness and eagerness. She endured school so she could retreat to her cottage and reflect on the events of the day. She did her extra weekend chores, endured family trips and helped me a little more - all to relax in privacy at the bottom of the house garden across from the chickens and a whole galaxy away from the family.

I don't believe she would have been able to express her individuality as she did had we stayed where we were in the city suburbs - though had we stayed, her complete unconventionality would not have been so pronounced. Yet for all the feeling revealed in her diaries, I cannot discover what caused her to feel this way. I know how she felt, but not why.

I cannot remember when I first began to notice Jo's behaviour changing. Perhaps because she was always so very different, the changes seemed to blend into her natural persona in such a way as to hide any real problems. I do remember receiving a phone call from Mr James, her teacher and the principal of the school some time before the end of the second term of her second year there. She would have been in grade seven at the time - preparing to enter high school and working hard as she always did. I was shocked to realise Mr James knew my daughter well enough to recognise unnatural behavioural patterns I as her mother did not.

Jo was beginning to fall asleep in class. On the surface, why should that be worrying? Mr James knew the home responsibilities Jo had, the increased homework load and possible pressure she was under. The main problem seemed to be that, while she fell asleep easily, in a mere two or three minutes, she would be in such a deep sleep that it was impossible to wake her without drawing the attention of the entire upper school. Jo's embarrassment was profound, and Mr James, being a sensitive teacher, tried to spare her that. I promised to look into the matter, but with one thing or the other, I completely forgot for a month or two. Besides, although Jo was going to bed much earlier, her chores were still being done, as was her homework.

When I allowed myself to think of it, I could see no problem, and concluded Mr James may have been at fault. Perhaps more interesting lessons were needed for her. Perhaps he could have given her a little more free reign in creative writing and art classes. Perhaps all she needed was a little mental stimulation. Perhaps I could shift the blame to someone else.

Then the holidays came, Jo's chores were still being done, and she spent her spare time in her cottage. I assumed everything was back to normal. How could I be so wrong?

It was about a month after these holidays I first noticed a dramatic change in Jo. She was definitely slackening off - her chores were not done in her usual quick and efficient way; she was snappy with her younger brothers; her young face was etched in lines I could not understand and she was not happy. She still spent her spare time on the roof under the fig tree and it was only after these spells in her sanctuary that she would resemble anything like her former self - though not for long. I also noticed that it was becoming increasingly difficult to arouse her from her reverie from the top of the roof, and when I did, her eyes were glazed and unfocused for a long time.

I was not ashamed to admit she was beginning to frighten me - not because I feared my safety around her, but because she was so distant and seemed so otherworldly. I confided in Jeremy then. He tried to alleviate my fears, and to a certain extent he was successful. However, there was still that niggling doubt that something I couldn't control was happening to my daughter.

I let it ride. I should have consulted a doctor, or a psychiatrist, or anyone. I didn't. Gradually, it became the norm for Jo to be snappy. Her happy moments were a God-send. We seemed to forget the old Jo for the new Jo had taken her place so completely.

It was about this time I thought she might be on drugs, so I searched her room. Nothing. I searched her cottage. Nothing. I was at a loss.

Then it was summer; the holidays began and the temperature rose. Somehow Jo seemed her usual self. I became more and more convinced school was the cause of all her troubles. I began to be grateful for the next few weeks when I could have my old Jo back and at the same time, I dreaded the start of a new school year a scant six weeks away. My mind convinced me the new and dreadful Jo would return with the first day of school. Christmas came and went, and still the temperature soared.

That fateful day started out ordinarily enough. Jo came in from the milking commenting on how hot it was. I had done what I could toward the day's meals. The bread dough was rising and breakfast was all set. The whole family had a wonderful meal together - lots of joking and tom-foolery that often accompanied the mealtimes of a large family. There was no hint of anything amiss.

It was the boys' turn to clean up after breakfast that day and since Jo's chores had been completed before breakfast, she was excused. As was normal for Jo, she retreated to her cottage. She was still there several hours later, happily sketching. The expression on her face was tranquil and her whole body glowed with a light of pure joy. I had never seen her so relaxed. I saw her sketch afterwards, and it has since been a source of comfort to me, but I had no idea of its importance and significance then. Jeremy needed her to slash the back paddock. Away from her cottage, the tractor was her next favourite place to be. Something to do with total solitude, I believe.

Jo always took a lot longer to do tractor chores than any other - possibly because she was not required to do them as often and relished the moments. She was not old enough to drive a motor car, of course, but driving a tractor on our property represented a total freedom for her. My older children from nine year old Harry to fifteen year old Samantha took their turns on the tractor, but Jo was the only one who really appreciated the freedom it provided. Plastered with sunblock and armed with sunhat, Jo took off, whistling tunelessly, for the wild, green yonder. She was gone for more than four hours before I began to worry. Even for Jo, that was a long time to do a quick slash of a two acre paddock.

Not wanting to alarm anyone, I left the house under the guise of seeking some solitude and headed off towards the back paddock. It was nearly midday and the temperature had been steadily rising. There was not a cloud in the sky to offer relief from the intense heat and the stark blueness and unrelenting glare were painful to my eyes. Still, I had to check on Jo.

I hadn't been able to see the tractor from the verandah, which wasn't unusual as the land undulated gently between the house and the paddock. What was more unsettling was that I couldn't hear the tractor, even as I approached the paddock. I told myself that the hills could mask the sound but as I climbed the last hill overlooking the paddock, the tractor was still nowhere in sight.

I stood for a moment, unsure of what to do next or where to start looking. The paddock was completely fenced. I stood by the gate, the only way in or out, apart from climbing the fence. I knew the children sometimes wandered further than the back fence, but no gate was needed there. I began to feel disoriented; my thoughts were wandering to irrelevant subjects; I wanted to focus on the situation at hand, but I didn't want to think where Jo could be.

Slowly I looked around the paddock. There were four boundaries: one through which I had entered the paddock; the far fence which was sparsely lined by tall gums; the border of the road; and the back fence. This fence was at the bottom of a small gully and was totally hidden from my view by a row of weeping willows. The other boundaries of the paddock were visible from where I was standing, and I could see nothing out of the ordinary there. I couldn't shake off the feeling of dread which had begun to overcome me when I started out to search for her. Jo was a big girl, I told myself. She could look after herself. These thoughts were getting me nowhere.

I sighed loudly, surveyed the paddock once more and started for the back fence. I needed to start somewhere. As I neared the gully, the feeling of dread grew stronger. I knew something bad had happened. The closer I came, the stronger the sense was and I began to run. I stopped short to catch my breath. I couldn't believe it. Jo was not there.

I think I panicked then. Memories of my subsequent actions were vague and distant. I must have found something because when I came to my senses, I was pummelling Jeremy's chest with my fists, my ashen face contorted with fear, screaming at him to find Jo, and when I stood back, there was blood all over his shirt. I remember staring horrified at the stains, and then I looked at my hands and found them covered in what appeared to be the same blood. Jeremy grabbed me roughly by the shoulders, shook me violently in a tried and true effort to knock some sense into me, and demanded to know what I had seen, and where. In a daze, I led him to the back fence.

There was the tractor, upended at the bottom of the gully and tangled in a web of barbed wires. Jeremy ran down to the tractor to see if there was any sign that Jo had even been there. He found a smeared pool of blood on a rock on the other side of the fence with a few strands of what appeared to be Jo's raven hair matted in it, but little else.

We could do nothing until we had called the police, but we would conduct our own search while we waited for them to arrive. Police thoroughly searched the area immediately around the tractor and for about a kilometre either side, paying particular attention to the neighbouring paddock, the gully and the creek that ran through it. For many hours, police and volunteers scoured the entire region. They even called in trackers who could also pick up no trace.

There were no tracks, or disturbances of any kind - apart from our own - or anything at all unusual, except in the vicinity of the upturned tractor. For all intents and purposes, Jo had been injured (police blood tests had since proven the blood was Jo's), and had just vanished.

They eventually called off the search. Police questioned each of us in turn, starting with me as it seems I could be considered a suspect. I had been the last to see her, and the first to find her gone. That really was the last straw for me. I loved my daughter. I couldn't hurt her. We simply couldn't find her.

When I could, I escaped to the relative sanctity of Jo's cottage. It was dark, but a golden moon shone through the gaping windows and doors, bathing the cottage in a haze of ethereal beauty. I held Jo's notebooks in my hand, unable to read them for the lack of light, but wanting to somehow understand Jo from them.

Jo's notebooks are still in her cottage. I often go there now, just to be near her. It's become a sort of shrine, somewhere to remember my daughter, somewhere to wait for the answer to her disappearance.

Pride of place on the only solid wall in the cottage

is the sketch Jo was working on the day she disappeared. I framed it a little while ago from some old wood from the Moreton Bay fig. It's a sketch of my Jo, eyes closed against the pain, an angelic expression on her face, rising above the world on wings of fire, being carried to the peace and sanctity she so desperately craved in her short life.

My home in the hills is no longer magical. I hate it here now and always will. But how can I leave? When I speak of my daughter it's as if she is dead. I think she must be. But I don't want to think of her as dead. I don't know where she is. Or if she died, I don't know how. She must be somewhere. Someone must know, surely. Nobody can just disappear like that.

Did you, Jo?

Point of View: It's all relative, really

REMORSE?

Why am I here, you ask.

It's a long story and normally I wouldn't tell anyone. But, seeing as it's you and you've asked so nicely... Let's see. Perhaps a little background will be enough...

Like everyone, I don't really know the beginning of my story. It happened before I was born. You see, there was this bloke and this broad – he was about 17 and she was 15. Jailbait, really, but her mother was known as the town bike and his dad never really recovered from the war, or to be more precise, his mother didn't recover from what he'd become because of the war, and so they hooked up and ... yada, yada, yada, some months later I was born.

(What??!!!! I beg your pardon, young man! I don't want to bore you with those details ... you cheeky monkey!)

Ahem … As I was saying, not long before I was born, they married, and not long after I was born, he passed away and left my mother alone. Nearly 17 she was and already a widow.

She was a pretty young thing then, or so I am told, and after a suitable period of mourning, had a long list of suitors. One of these turned out to be a very unsavoury character, who even served time for paedophilia, I understand, and one was a cripple. Not that I have anything against people with disabilities, and really, look at me! Who am I to talk?

Anyway, apparently, and this is only hearsay as I have no recollection of this, he used to get me to fetch and carry for him all the time. My mother felt that she didn't want me to be used as a slave (rather ironic, as you will later see) and so she called that one off. I can't believe she nearly married him!

I was about four, I suppose, when she finally found someone she thought she could marry.

He was a handsome Irishman. At least, his father was Irish and his mother was German, and to my mother, he appeared to be the answer to all her dreams. We became a 'happy family' and I had a new daddy. Since I never knew the first one, I accepted the second one as the only one, and even took on his name.

He was a hard worker, and my mother enjoyed playing house while he was out working all day, looking after me and the other children who eventually came along. He'd come home to an immaculate house and dinner ready, although this perfection slipped a little the more children they had.

I've jumped ahead here. Sorry.

In the early days, when it was just me, my new daddy would take my mother and me for drives in the country. We'd drive for miles, just taking in the scenery, and stopping somewhere for a picnic. Sounds idyllic, doesn't it? On one of these days, we were driving through a valley alongside a winding river and 'daddy' decided we should stop off at the dam further up the river to have a look. I was excited to see the dam. It was like a swear word that I was allowed to say: Dam, Dam, Dam, I'd chant, over and over.

It was beautiful. The lake side was gorgeous and lined with the bush. Giant eucalyptus gums towered above me and the quicker growing pines gave off their scent in the warm air.

'Let's walk along the dam wall!' he said, and so we did

It was cold concrete, wide enough to feel safe, until you went to the edge and looked over. It was so far down and I was so scared. And then on the other side, there were these dark, gaping holes with flimsy grates over them, and, coming up from them, I could hear the roar of the water being let out of the chute. The dam doubles as a hydro-electric power plant. I remember clinging to my mother's hand and then, horror of horrors, my daddy wanted us to pose for a photo!

'Over there!' he said, pointing to the gaping mouth of the giant with the grizzly monstrous roar.

(What! You think I'm exaggerating? Please bear in mind I was only a little over four and very tiny.)

I remember screaming, begging him not to make me stand there.

'The monsters will get me!' I cried, but my tears had no effect on the monster that stood in front of me. I was trapped. Monsters behind and a monster in front, nowhere was safe, but I had to choose.

'Smile, dammit!' my stepfather ordered.

I found that photo the other day and nearly shook with fear at the mere memory it evoked. Not a happy family snap, I can assure you. A very tearful, fearful grimace in the place of a smile, but he was happy.

Sorry? Yes. Well. I am getting to that...

As the years went by, he and my mother had more children. In fact about a year or so after they married my brother was born, then fourteen months later, my sister, and then eighteen months after that, my second brother. I was now seven, in my second or third year of school and already a dab hand at ironing, washing dishes, folding clothes, cleaning the bathroom, sweeping floors, making beds, even changing babies' nappies. They should have called me Cinders! They had two more girls after that, too, and the chores mounted up.

And as if that wasn't bad enough, if the jobs

weren't done well enough, I felt the full brunt of his anger. He wasn't a very big man – well, now I can look back and see that, but I was a small child and to me he towered frighteningly over me. And he didn't just use his hand. I would've almost forgiven that, but he used to grab whatever he could lay his hands on and lay into me with that – a belt (studded or with a huge metal buckle like the cowboys wear), sticks, broom handles, riding crop, once even the business end of an electric fryer cord. Man! That one left a massive bruise and quite a few cuts as well – and like always, it was on the back of my thighs, high enough up so that the teacher couldn't have seen them for the length of my skirts.

You know, I often wondered how my teachers never knew, though. I mean, tell me, if you saw a kid come into school and wince as she slowly lowers herself to her hard, wooden seat, you'd ask questions, wouldn't you?

No? Ah! Whatever!

Where was I? Oh, yeah. I think I finally understood my place in the family on my mother's birthday the year I turned 12. We'd been out for a meal, I think, and she must've still been quite young, so maybe that can excuse what she did.

Anyway, we'd just got home from this dinner, or whatever, and, at this time we were living on a ten-acre farm – at least, I thought of it as a farm and really, I loved it there – lots of work, but lots of hiding places, too.

Where was I? Oh yeah! We just got home from dinner and hadn't milked the cows yet so he sent me out in the pitch dark to get them in so I could milk them. Although I was nearly a grown-up 12, I was, well, kinda okay with the dark if there was someone big with me, or if I had a torch, but this time, I wasn't allowed one and I was alone.

And there're cane toads and all sorts of things that jump out of the fields at night in the country and I felt sick with fear. I had to go out in the dark on my own, without a torch, and bring the damned cows in.

I went yahoo-ing across the old wheat field – which is where the cows were – climbed through the barbed wire fence, carefully, I might add, and ran to the neighbours' house to borrow a torch. Well, as you may be able to appreciate, I had scared these cows to the gate which is where my brother found them, placid as you like, chewing their cuds like they'd been there all along.

Man, did I get it when I got back inside! He let fly with everything he had. I was black and blue from a-hole to breakfast hole.

And my mother got in the car and drove away.

That was the worst he ever did, but after that, he didn't have to do anything anymore. I did everything he asked, and everything I thought he was going to ask, always thinking I was going to get it if it wasn't good enough, and often it wasn't.

Anyway, he and my mother divorced after I left

home and he married a woman with lots of young kids. I saw him slam the phone into the youngest girl's face. It was just because she wouldn't hang up on her friend immediately he asked her to.

I was visiting them – some sort of misplaced sense of duty, because he was dying. Cancer.

After he'd done it and gone out, I hugged the poor child and told her not to worry. He'd never hurt her again. She was sobbing so much and I don't know if she heard. She wouldn't have believed me anyway. I know if someone had said the same to me, I wouldn't have believed them.

Anyway, that night he died. His wife had been working all day so she was tired. In the morning she said he'd made some strange gurgling noise in the middle of the night and she told him to shut up, roll over and go back to sleep. I didn't think she saw me.

I didn't cry at his funeral. I didn't plan to do what I did, but I wasn't sorry, either. I'm still not, if the truth be told.

So. Well. Now you know why I'm here. Still think you can help me get out?

Point of View: It's all relative, really

POINT OF VIEW

Liberty

I don't remember ever crying before, but today, my tears flowed as freely as the dust that floated on the breeze and wafted across the harbour to my island sanctuary. O that my tears would be enough to wash away the misery! Alas! It was not to be.

I am alone, alone in my misery. The rest of the world can comfort each other, but my family has been gone for many a year. There is no one left. Yes, the birds of the air are my friends. They only require that I provide for them somewhere to rest, and occasionally they beg for food. I give to them and they are satisfied.

Far below my home I look upon the sea. I am surrounded by sea, that foaming green instigator of all life. The sea gulls dive gracefully, cavorting and swooping as they swim. They race each other and noisily fight over morsels of food they find in their travels. I am constantly surprised by the harshness of their voices. I always feel such graceful creatures should sing, not scream with raucous rancour at the world. Maybe they know something I don't.

The sea creatures swim around me, and press their bodies close for comfort and camaraderie. From a lofty height, I gaze down at them, pouring my love out to them. We are great friends. To them, I simply am.

I understand most of the creatures I see daily. They fight to eke out an existence, never taking more than they need, and killing only as necessary.

But Man. Him I do not understand! Today, I saw what Man could do. And for the first time in my life, I wept.

Looking out to sea, I spy some ships heading for the harbour. Their passage tosses a foamy wake behind them, but to me in my lofty tower, it looks like a mere ripple. Sometimes I tire of the view to the front and long to see something else. Today was such a day, and so I looked toward the city. It's Fall and too early in the season to be cold. A cool crisp breeze flutters about my feet, sending an errant leaf on a flight towards the edge of the island.

I am old now, and can no longer turn my head, but my eyes are good. If I glance sideways I can see that glorious Manhattan skyline. It is beautiful, with its towers and skyscrapers stretching toward the heavens. Only Man could build something so beautiful.

It was like a dream. A plane crosses the city – they don't usually do that, but I am not concerned. I look away for a brief moment as a bird lands on my arm clutching a precious crumb in its beak. It sings a sweet song for me: the crumb flutters unheeded to my feet.

A movement catches my eye. I glance back to the city. My eyes are riveted on the scene unfolding before me. I find it hard to believe, but it is true. The plane crashes into one of the towers and erupts in a ball of flame. I can feel a perceptible rise in temperature, even from here. A tear squeezes its way out of my crusty old eyes and streaks my cheek as it washes years of grime from my face.

My vision is blurred now and as the minutes tick by the hazy scene burns into my memory. And then comes the unthinkable sequel. Another plane crashes into the second tower. My grief knows no bounds. My heart breaks as I hear the cries of thousands of people. They don't stand a chance of surviving, those in the planes and those in the top floors of the towers.

Then all is silent.

And yet I stand. I no longer try to look toward the city. My father made me to look to the sea, to welcome people to the land of Liberty. That I can do, standing stoically, standing proud. I cannot be destroyed, or if I, too, am reduced to rubble, like the two towers, yet will I live on in the memory of each and every free man, woman and child who live in this land.

I am Liberty. I light the way to freedom and peace, and what I stand for can never be destroyed.

Michelle

I'm late again. I don't know what's wrong with me, but I've been late every day this week. I'll lose my job. I'm so tired. I've got to hurry! I park the car, get out and slam the door. Still, I love New York. It's so busy and Fall is just the best season of the year. It's cool enough, without being too cold, and it's pretty, too.

There's a gentle breeze drifting down the streets, as clean as any city air can be. It's still early, yet already the city is bustling with renewed life and energy. I think I just need a holiday. Then everything will be all right again.

I walk through the glass doors, check the notice board for messages, and slink past the Brad, the shift supervisor's desk to the clock. Just when I think I've made it, his foghorn of a voice booms out.

"Michelle," he roars, "you're late again."

I shrug my shoulders, stifle a yawn and promise it won't happen again. He nods and I'm on my way. I'm not that late, anyway. I was due in at 8:00 and it's now 8:30. Big deal. It's only half an hour. The traffic was horrendous, and I just can't face the underground. One day I'll face my fear of enclosed spaces, but not today. Not now.

Upstairs in the tearoom, my colleagues are already sipping on hot coffee. I pour myself a cup and settle down to hear the latest goss. Brad interrupts our session, and hands out assignments. I expected to be on desk duty again, but today there's a change. I'm on foot patrol, and with my partner, Rod, we set off.

We're about a block from the World Trade Centre, which is where we'll probably centre our activities for the morning. Tourists flood the area, so it's a great place for undesirables to hang out. It's still a beautiful morning and I'll have to thank Brad for sending me out here. I don't feel so tired, now.

There's so much paper lying around. It looks just like the old war movies when bombers drop propaganda on unsuspecting cities. Someone's going to have to clean up this mess.

There's a bit of a commotion further on. Rod and I go into automatic mode.

I radio the station to let them know there's a problem, as per protocol, and then Rod and I run towards the scene.

It's pandemonium. Some people are staring up at the sky. Others are running; panic painting an eerie mask on their faces. I'm confused. I follow the upward gaze of those rooted to the spot, and gasp in horror.

There's a plane sticking out near the top of the one of the Towers and smoke and flames are billowing out.

"Oh, my God," I say, shock holding me still for a moment.

Then training kicks in and both Rod and I go to work. Rod reports the incident while I direct the people away from the Centre. I can see people streaming from the building and I hope someone is in there to keep them moving. It's such a long way down, and the elevators may not be safe. They'll only be used for extreme cases.

I go on automatic pilot, directing people away, waiting for orders from the boss via Rod. *Oh, those poor people,* I think to myself. *There must be hundreds above the floors that are burning who'll have no way of escaping.*

I try not to think of them, as I help those shaken people leave the Centre.

Rod comes towards me and tells me we're to go inside and help coordinate the evacuation. The boss is on his way down here, as is the Mayor.

A movement catches my attention and I look up. I can't believe it! There's another plane headed for the other Tower. Surely not! My heart leaps into my throat then falls back to beat a painful tattoo in my chest. I take a deep breath and slowly exhale.

Oh, God. Not again.

This one seems to hit down lower. There's more people trapped on the floors above. What hope do they have? Someone screams beside me. I think it's a delayed reaction to the horror but then I look to where she's pointing. There're people jumping from those floors above the crash site. What are they thinking? Surely they don't think they can make it from that high? I want to catch them but I know it's useless.

I run inside. Rod follows close behind. We've got to get people moving. The urgency hits. By now emergency services teams are all over the place. More cops have joined us and firemen are already making their way up inside the Towers. Paramedics are treating people for shock, or encouraging them to move on.

It's chaos, but it's ordered. I know that sounds crazy but that's how it seems. People are running in every direction. There's people leaving the buildings and there's emergency services workers running in. People are shouting to each other, encouraging and directing each other. It's utter madness – not what we're doing, but the fact we have to do something.

I don't know how long I've been in here, but I get the feeling I've got to get out. It's like the feeling I had once when Dad made me and my brothers climb into a cave, just to see what was there. My brothers had a ball. I was terrified. I felt like that now.

"Rod, I've got to get out of here!" I scream at him. He knows my problem, but doesn't understand why it's here, now. Neither do I. He shakes his head at me, but I can't stay. I turn towards the exit and then I hear this incredible groaning. It's like the building is protesting. I stop dead in my tracks, as does everyone else. Then realisation dawns on me. The building is collapsing.

I scream at the top of my lungs, and, like a madwoman, I rush at the people still standing there.

"Get out of here! Run!" I shout and start to bulldoze them on their way. Rod must have realised what was happening the same time I did. I see him doing the same thing, waving his truncheon at people like he's trying to hit them, when all the while he's herding them out the door.

We run. We all run.

I see nothing except for the open space outside the building and the people I'm shepherding out. We have to get out.

Somehow I make it clear of the tumbling debris. The air is thick with dust and I can hardly breathe. It's in my hair, on my clothes, up my nose and even in my mouth. My eyes are watering, trying to wash it out. It's disgusting, but I'm alive. I draw my shirt up around my mouth and breathe in deep. Oh, bad mistake. The dust is so fine it penetrates the open spaces in the fabric and I collapse in a fit of coughing. I'll be more careful in future.

Slowly the dust settles and I look around.

"Rod!" I scream. I can't see him. But he was right behind me, I'm sure. Other cops are trying to tell me to get out of there; to leave the vicinity; to just get somewhere safe. But my partner is missing. I have to find him.

I turn back, but a burly fireman obstructs my path. I struggle against this gorilla that holds me captive, mustering all my strength. I break free and run into the danger zone. There's no one there. Wildly I look around. I try to climb the mound that was the Tower, but my would-be protector catches up with me.

"There's people in there!" I scream, but my voice is hoarse.

"We've got to get out of here!" he yells at me, and I know he's right. I can sense, rather than hear, the second Tower groaning.

"But I've got to go back."

He lifts me bodily and runs with me as fast as he can. I try again to break free, but it's no use. My energy is spent. I can't win.

I go limp in his arms and he gently lowers me to the pavement. There's dust everywhere. The place looks like something out of a nightmare. It is a nightmare.

Slowly, I lower my head. I hug my knees tightly to my chest and rest my head on my arms. I can't believe it's happened; yet here I am. I saw it. Great sobs rack my body as reality strikes at the core of my being. I want revenge. I will find a way to avenge my partner's death.

I raise my tear-streaked face heavenward. God help me, but I won't take this lying down.

Jules and Jack

My phone rings as I'm about to rush out the door. The children are unusually reluctant to go to school today, so we're a little late leaving. To tell the truth, I slept in, and we're very late leaving. I'm tempted to just let it ring, I mean, everyone who knows me knows I need to rush out the door at this time. Still, there's urgency in the tone. I reach for the receiver and the phone goes dead. I've wasted precious moments in my indecision.

I turn to once again hurry the children into the car, and the phone rings again. I am closer now, so angrily, I reach for the receiver.

"Yes?" I say, imperiously, into the receiver. My tone is not welcoming and reflects my agitated state of mind.

"Honey, thank God you're still home," says my husband's voice. I can't believe it! Jack of all people knows my morning schedule and it's on his account I'm so rushed today. He's arriving home from a business trip shortly, and I have to drive out to the airport to pick him up, after I drop the children at school. And I wanted to fit in a beauty parlour appointment beforehand, you know, to scrub away the drudge of the past few weeks while he's been gone.

"Jack, I'm just about to rush out the door..." I begin, but he cuts me off.

"Honey, the plane's been hijacked. They say

there's a bomb on board."

A buzzing fills my head and I go weak all over. I can't think straight. He'll be home soon. What kind of a joke is this? I sink to the floor, gripping the phone as if my very life depended on it. Somehow I knew my husband's did. I felt powerless.

"Oh, God, Jack." My voice is a whisper. "Please don't do anything stupid." But even as I'm speaking, he whispers to me his plan.

"Some of us think we can jump these guys," he says. "We've got to do something. Someone up front overheard them talking. They're heading for the White House. God, Jules, we've got to stop them."

I want to keep him talking, but I don't know what to say. I pray in my heart that they'll be safe. But it's an empty prayer.

"Uh, Jack, Don't be a hero. Leave that for the younger studs, eh." I try to keep my voice light, but it cracks, just a little bit. I swallow hard.

"Jack, I love you. You've got to come home."

"Babe..." He hasn't called me that since we were dating. "I need you to be strong for me. Time's running out. We've got to stop them, or it's all over."

My eyes wander to the TV. I forgot we'd turned it on. *Just as well Jack called. Now I can turn it off before I leave.* I start over to the set, and then stop. *What am I doing? My husband's in danger and all I can think about is turning the stupid TV off.* It seems so unreal.

There's some early movie playing about planes hitting the Trade Centre Towers. Funny, I thought I was up on all the movies, but I've never heard of this one.

Oh, my God. It's real.

"Jack," I say, panic beginning to register in my voice. "The World Trade Centre's been hit. Oh God, by two planes full of people."

There's silence on the other end, then I hear Jack's urgent whisper. I can't make out what he's saying until I realise he's not speaking to me.

"Babe," he now says into the phone," I need you to do something for me. I need you to call the newspaper and tell them what's happening here. They'll follow it up. In the meantime, stay with the kids. I'll call you back in five minutes."

He severs the connection. Numbly, I call the newspaper and relay my husband's message to them. I don't think they believe me. I hope they do.

"Jenny! Paul! Mickey! Come here!" I call out to my children. They come grumbling in, but something in my face stops them in their tracks.

"Hey, kids," I say, gently now, "Daddy's going to call us from the plane."

I forgot about the TV again, and Jenny is staring at it. News reporters are on the scene giving a blow-by-blow account of the tragedy.

"It seems so real," she says.

"It is," I quietly tell her. She turns to me like a startled deer, horror written all over her ten-year-old face. "Daddy!" she whispers, knowing her Daddy is at that very moment on a plane home.

"He's not there," I tell her and I see the relief flood her face. *Oh, God,* I pray, *how can I bare this? How can I tell my children they may never see their father again?* I struggle within myself to regain control.

The phone rings.

I pounce on it.

"Hello?" I can barely breathe, but I force the word out.

"Jules, it's me again."

"Say Hi to the kids," I tell him.

I hand the phone to Jenny.

"Hi Daddy," she says. She listens for a bit, whispers: "I love you too, Daddy. I miss you." Her voice breaks and she hands the phone to Paul.

"Hi," he says. Jack talks to Paul for a little longer and then he talks to Mickey. Mickey hands the phone back to me, and my three little babies sit around me in a circle, their faces white and solemn. My heart aches for them.

"Jack, I'm back," but he knows it's me.

"Jules..." there's a long pause and I can hear a heavy sigh. "It's decided. We're going to stop them, one way or another. It's a good plan. We should be

OK. I'm going to leave the phone line open, so you can hear our success." I know he's trying to convince himself, as much as me. I hear someone say, "It's now or never," then Jack tells me goodbye. He says he loves me, and no matter what, I'm to remember that always. I understand he has to do something. I know he's going to die, but I don't want his death to be in vain. Perhaps I'm wrong and they'll gain control of the plane, but I don't think so.

"I love you," I whisper, and then I hear the thud as the phone drops. I slowly sink to the floor.

My heart is thudding as my ear, glued to the phone, hears the sounds of struggle. I hear Jack's voice, and the muffled voices yelling in a foreign language.

"We're going into the field!" I hear someone close to the phone yell. There are terrified screams, and I can hear a few prayers. Finally, an explosion. Then, nothing.

Still I sit with my ear pressed to the phone, hoping to hear Jack; hoping to hear anyone, I don't care. But there's nothing. I stare sightlessly at the TV, not registering the scenes unfolding before my eyes. New York is a tragedy, but it's not my tragedy. My husband was coming home; now he's lost to me forever. I feel as if my heart is breaking.

"Mom?" Jenny moves to sit beside me. She presses her little hands to my face and gently turns me to look at her. I see her, but through the haze of my tears.

"Mom, we'll be OK," she says. "Daddy said so."

I let go, then. My grief flows like a torrent. My poor children! My poor husband! What am I to do? Silently, I gather my children to me and we sit in a solemn circle of love. I don't know what the future holds for us, but I do know we have each other. And nobody can take that away from us.

George W

A terrible tragedy has befallen the American people today. And it's not just the American people. This event affects the whole free world. We will stand up to terrorism. We will show them we are strong. When Pearl Harbour was attacked, we fought back and grew stronger. We'll fight back again.

We'll flush out the terrorists, wherever they may be hiding, and bring them to justice. There will be nowhere they can go to hide. And any person or nation or country that harbours or protects them can expect the same fate. If you're not with us, you're against us. We will avenge the deaths of the innocent who lost their lives today, September 11.

America is the symbol of freedom – the personification of Liberty. Our forefathers founded this great nation of ours as a refuge from tyranny. We will not be intimidated into giving up our freedom. We will not allow them to think they can break us. We will not stop until we have rid the world of every ounce of terrorism. We will not be beaten.

Freedom will prevail.

POETRY

FOUR SEASON SONNETS

SPRING

There's freshness in the air with just a taste
Of warmth to take the Winter chill away.
A gentle night-time drizzle cleans her face
While wispy clouds race o'er the springtime sky.
A brilliant cloak of colour hides the stare
Of winter. Jacaranda's purple flow'rs
Adorn the limbs of trees once grey and bare
With scented air to drown in hour by hour.
Birds sing at dawn with crystal note so sweet;
A melody, well-carried on the breeze.
And new-hatched young await the morning treat
While nestled, safe in tops of swaying trees.
Small creatures from long Winter sleep awoke
To see a world renewed with joy and hope.

SUMMER

A seasoned heat, the bright sun bakes the ground

And saps all land of moisture, giving birth

To death. Fierce fire, and fiercer winds abound,

And grip once-fertile land in want and dearth.

Thin cattle, parched and listless mill around.

Ripe melons shrivel. Tendrils grasp the earth,

Curl up and die when sustenance not found

In arid land. A measure of man's worth.

The dams give up their water to the skies

Who greed'ly lap it up, and selfish hold

Until, the weight remains aloft no more.

Black, laden clouds, upon th'horizon rise

To shift the season. Grass turns green from gold

And Nature once again evens the score.

AUTUMN

Long cycle at the turning point of time
Where green leaves' subtle changes solve the rhyme
Of Birth and Death and what lies in between,
Of reds, of golds and glorious Autumn scenes.
While days grow shorter, longer nights grow cool
And overnight ice forms upon the pool.
Ma Earth slows down, prepares herself for rest -
Puts on a show – example of her best.
Wild animals conclude their daylight task
Of gath'ring food before the winter fast.
Preparing dens for refuge from the cold
Excessive hunger makes small creatures bold
Enough to brave impending Winter's gloom,
To save young families from eternal doom.

WINTER

Lo! See the snows upon the hallowed ground.

It gently smoothes the lines of death and strife.

Stark limbs e'er stretching – they are heaven-bound –

Displaying death, but hinting promised life.

Lo! Whistling winds create a haunting sound.

They play the cracks in log walls like a fife,

And stripping warmth from people gathered 'round

As icy tendrils slice thru' like a knife.

But winter in Australia's not like this.

Tho' cold it gets, the snows will seldom come.

A heavy frost may form upon the land,

As cold air gives the dew an icy kiss.

Or winter rains on iron rooftops drum

A steady beat for Nature's marching band.

DISCOVERING THE LIGHT

Alone, I sit outside the orb of light

Afraid to enter, lest by ent'ring find

Myself – a sad and sorry soul who might

Awaken to the absence of my mind.

An edge of darkness closes out the view

I might have used to look beyond my life

Upon this sphere. I want to live the truth

But find myself embroiled in pain and strife.

Yet stepping bravely from the dark to light

I leave behind my fears instead to trust

The bearer of the Light which holds my heart.

There's one who's greater, full of pow'r and might,

Who bears the cross, an ensign to the just,

And aids me while he plays the bigger part.

UNQUENCHABLE FIRE

A fire's burning deep within my heart -
So deep I feel I cannot let it out.
It fights for air to breathe and show the part
I hide. I want to scream and shout.
A passion rides the wave of sanity
That keeps me ever grounded on the earth
'Til overwhelmed by my own vanity
Those feelings in my heart show my true worth.
There is a fire. It burns within my breast.
For what the fire burns I must not tell.
I wish my tears could put the fire out
And lift the aching burden from my chest,
For then the longed-for joy could fin'lly swell -
A sweet crescendo. Yea, a joyful shout.

Phoebe Wilby

RECONCILIATION

Please don't blame me

If my words are not your words;

My ways are not your ways;

My skin is different to yours.

Understand I wasn't there

When your lands were sold for nothing;

Your children taken from you

To live a 'better way'.

I never introduced you to the white man's demon
drink;

The deadly cancer sticks;

Gross illness and the plague.

I cannot be sorry for things I did not do;

I wouldn't expect it of you –

Why expect it then, of me?

Yet even if my ancestors had done these things

To your ancestors,

Why blame me?

I wasn't there.

It wasn't me.

And it wasn't done to you.

That's not to say I'm not sorry

For what happened to your people,

For what my people did to your people,

Or for what our people did to their own.

But it must be a past memory.

The future lies ahead.

We have to live together.

Why worry about a little word?

It means nothing if I have done nothing to be sorry
for,

And you were not the person wronged.

But I am sorry.

I'm sorry we cannot forget the past.

I'm sorry we cannot look to the future.

I'm sorry we have to try to compensate you

For what our ancestors did to your ancestors.

Where does it end? Know this –

Some of my ancestors are your ancestors, too.

We're all of the same blood.

Let's be reconciled

To that.

Phoebe Wilby

ESSAYS

ALL FOR ONE – DIVERSITY IN THE MODERN WORLD

We live in a troubled world. In terms of wealth and resources, great inequalities exist between nations. We're materialistic and depend on technology for our creature comforts. We're egocentric; so long as our needs are met, there is no need to look to others for assistance. We are rapidly depleting our earth's natural resources and failing to put back what we take out. As a resul,t our world is unhealthy, and many of its inhabitants are unhealthy also. But there is enough, and to spare, for each and every one of us. The answer lies in recognising the talents and special attributes of individuals and nations, learning to get along with each other, and educating each other in the use of natural resources and technologies to assist in day-to-day living.

While researching this topic, I was appalled at the

economic emphasis placed by wealthy nations on the giving of aid to famine-riddled, and less developed countries. There appeared to be a very real fear that if nations were offered, for example, whole wheat at reduced prices, it would artificially deflate the price gotten elsewhere. Where this is a concern for those who make their living on the land, most of the profits did not go to the primary producer, but to big business and conglomerates set up to regulate the industry. Consequently, great stores of wheat and other grains, as well as vegetables, rotted in warehouses and storage facilities, rather than be given at heavily subsidised prices to needy nations.

Therefore, I concluded that the issue of "to genetically modify or not to genetically modify" was a moot point. Developing nations, while "technologically disadvantaged", nevertheless have a lot to offer the world economy. We're all brothers and sisters under the same sun and need to treat each other that way.

I was out driving to recharge my car battery after one of my children left the doors open overnight, and happened upon an unfamiliar country road a scant ten minutes from my home. The diversity of the shrubbery and the untamed beauty of the countryside beside which I was driving struck a chord with me. I'm not a city slicker, by any means, though I do live in a fairly highly populated suburb. Yet this scenery was a tonic to my soul. Do we need nature? Perhaps many would think not, but in just a few short minutes driving down a country lane, I once again caught a glimpse, in only a small way, of the importance of nature in my life.

My early childhood was spent in the city but with nomadic parents, we naturally moved a lot. One such move was to an isolated farming community in the Brisbane Valley where we were the proud owners of a ten-acre lot complete with an old farmhouse. It was mostly grassland with a few trees, but with hard work and great industry, we soon transformed it into a profitable concern. The profit was not in money, but in our ability to live off its produce.

One acre was under wheat and another under lucerne. We milked a couple of cows, kept what seemed like hundreds of chickens and generally grew what fruits and vegetables we needed. We used bore water for irrigation and washing, tank water for drinking, and generally recycled vegetable scraps either as compost for the garden or chicken feed. The chickens not only provided us with eggs and meat occasionally, but also provided a great source of fertilizer for our passionfruit! To pay basic utilities and other running expenses, my father sold fish and painted houses. For other things, there was the barter system.

It was a hard life, but very rewarding – and not that long ago at all. My own children have experienced nothing of the life I led, and though they are still young I mourn for their loss. We live, for the most part, in a world of ease and selfishness. At the flick of a switch, we have light. We open the refrigerator and there is food; supermarket shelves abound with ready-to-eat meals; clothes come off the racks. But a life of luxury and ease comes at a terrific price and great loss. Although the loss of skills gained from husbandry and cottage industry is great, the loss to the gene pool and the environment is even greater.

Fast-growing, disease- and drought-resistant varieties of grains and vegetables have the potential to help third world countries overcome their food crisis – but are they simply a band-aid solution to a wider reaching problem, and are these solutions a problem within themselves? Even the scientific community is divided on these issues.

Some scientists warn that genetically engineered food may have serious long-term health and environmental consequences, even going so far as to claim that utilising them may "worsen chances of food security in the developing world". These claims are based on the explanation that normal gene functions are extremely tightly controlled to ensure that organisms and all their inherent characteristics are produced in the correct order, as nature intended.

The genetic modifications occurring naturally are as a result of cross-pollination between closely related species, also occurring naturally. By developing these resistant strains, we are limiting the gene pool and thus risking the extinction of an entire species of necessary foods in the human food chain, should a crop become infected by a virus or such other unforeseen pestilence. To assume this is impossible is both naïve and ignorant. The potato famine in Ireland between 1845 and 1852 is testament to the fact that a simple disease has the potential to wipe out the entire harvest of a nation's crops, causing the starvation of entire communities and sometimes, even death.

On the other hand, scientists working on the genetic modification programmes claim these hybrid varieties, being resistant to disease and requiring less water to grow, have the potential to be a boon to developing countries, allowing them to produce their own food to feed their own population, and thus allow them to be self-sufficient.

Though I see merit in both arguments, I would like to see an entirely different approach to the growing food crisis of the world. I believe there is the means to produce abundant food and enough to spare on this planet, to feed every man, woman and child for many years to come. Although the land, in many places, is depleted of both water and the nutrients necessary to grow healthy and nutritious grains, vegetables and animals for food, other lands have abundant tracts of arable land. Humankind has the knowledge and capability to replenish the earth – to give back to nature what man has taken, as it were – and thus provide the entire world population with the nourishment we all need.

The "Oil-for-Food Programme (OIP)" operating

from 1995 to 2003 between oil-rich Middle-Eastern countries and agriculturally-rich western countries such as the United States and parts of Europe, is a mere drop in the ocean of what we can accomplish. Repairing agricultural lands by returning nutrients to the soil, building up what is already in place and accepting another country's contribution to the well-being of our own is, in my opinion, the answer.

Yes, I am proposing a return to the barter system – modified to suit modernity, but a system to allow regions to utilise what they already have to obtain what they need. Instead of trying to irrigate an arid land such as Ethiopia where rainfall has forgotten to fall for many years, why not turn to solar power as an exportable commodity for this country? Sunshine is abundantly available – so much so that crops dry and die before they have a chance to blossom. Areas such as the fertile Nile Valley can provide food in return for electrical power. We therefore have an expensive commodity in the form of food and water exchanged for solar power, a renewable, never-ending and certainly ecologically sound natural resource. Countries such as Australia are rich in minerals and natural resources (renewable or otherwise) and produce excesses in food and other necessary provisions for modern comfort. The temptation for nations such as this to push self-reliance, ignoring for the most part the needs of their neighbours, serves no one but themselves and should be openly discouraged by Earth's inhabitants as a whole.

For this modern barter system to become a viable

alternative we not only need to recognise the value of biodiversity in nature, we also need to recognise the value of "biodiversity" in humanity. Just as all nations have something valuable to contribute to the well-being of the earth and its inhabitants, so too, do all individuals. Yet the inequalities existing between the peoples of the earth are widening. There are too many poor among us; the wealthy few control the majority of the land and resources. We may be tempted to believe this only occurs in countries such as India which still operates under the caste system, or Ethiopia where famine has ravaged the land for many years, but this is not so. It also happens in so-called Western societies where free enterprise is supposed to guarantee a fair go for all.

What is it that prevents humanity from working together? Is it a lack of funds? Is it a lack of care? Or is it an indifference to the suffering of others? I do not have these answers, but there is one thing I do know. We desperately need nature; in fact we cannot survive without it.

We need to use what we already have – refined to reflect the growing need to protect our earth and everything on it. Instead of spending money on weapons of destruction – mass or otherwise, why not divert the funds to developing cheaper alternatives to solar power. Education on conservation of fossil and non-renewable fuels is more important than developing a way to create more wealth for already wealthy nations. It is a sick world that places a high monetary value on a product that contributes so highly to greenhouse gas emissions – yet cannot address the problems of feeding its billions of inhabitants.

Wars are fought over oil; people die for oil; yet the oil will be depleted. On the other hand, this earth abounds in renewable resources. The source of power is freely available to many, though the harnessing of that power requires great technology. Let us develop and freely share this technology so that the power of the Sun is available to all.

There is power in diversity. There is power in knowledge. There is power in unity. When all the world works together, there is power.

Maybe we can't all go back to living on the land. Maybe we can't be totally self-sufficient and provide everything for ourselves, our families or our countries. We've come too far to go back to the post-modern era. Our parents' luxuries are our necessities. Those items we deem luxuries will become necessities for our children and our children's children, but we don't have to have these things at the expense of the world we live in.

Modern technology has a lot to answer for, but modern technology can also be the answer. We have natural resources at our disposal. The diversity of cultures dictates that all have something valuable to contribute to the overall well-being of our planet. There is no need for genetic modification of seeds and vegetables, as poorer countries have something to contribute to even the wealthiest nations in return for what they cannot provide for themselves. The wealthiest nations can release their stranglehold on the world economy and commodities and recognise the valuable input of every nation. Individually, we can take the steps to unite the world as one.

As one we can heal our planet, celebrate the diversity of nature and help to create a better world for us all.

February 2002

Point of View: It's all relative, really

CAN WE HAVE TOO MUCH SECURITY?

Big Brother is here, but what can we do to protect our freedom while maintaining our security?

In the wake of September 11, 2001, society has gone awry. The noose of world security is tightening. Bush's War on Terror is moving forward and gaining momentum. Governments are rushing legislation through their various parliaments to protect their citizens. These same acts of legislation are erasing, or have the potential to erase, the rights and freedoms of the citizens. The threat of terror has caused otherwise sane citizens to allow governments to exercise greater power over them. More and more of our personal information finds its way into databases either commissioned, or sanctioned, by those same governments. Law enforcement bodies want national and perhaps international databases with personal information, including DNA coding, of suspected and known criminals. In short, the world powers want YOUR information to use as they see fit.

But with this knowledge, your basic personal information has the potential to fall into the wrong hands. Do you want to be bombarded with advertising, just because some government department sold your information to the highest bidder? And unwanted contact from businesses is at the tame end of the scale. With the new technology currently available, your very identity is in jeopardy. In a world where everything is available on computers or the Internet if you just know where to look, nothing is sacred. Your personality can undergo a computer facelift. Any hacker could tap into our file and presto!! a law-abiding citizen becomes a fugitive. It's not just in Hollywood where personal identities are at risk. It is here in the real world, too. We all value our freedom.

We do not have to give up our freedom for security. We do not have to give up security to have freedom. Freedom is security, and if personal and individual responsibility is the doorway, education is the key.

INFORMATION IS POWER. World-wide, Governments seek to control their citizens through gathering and hoarding knowledge. Vast databases continue to grow as they gorge on facts and figures entered in by various government agencies. When governments exercise control over their citizens, there is no individual freedom; the people have no power.

No one in the free world could condone the violence against the United States' citizens on September 11. Nor would they condone similar violence against their own country, and no one in the free world would expect the man behind the crime to go unpunished. However, no one should be willing to trade their current freedoms for dubious securities which claim to safeguard against similar acts of terrorism while imposing unnecessary restrictions on law abiding citizens.

In 1997, the Cato Institute's Solveig Singleton, referring to Orwell's "1984", wrote: "Big Brother is an icon of totalitarianism more familiar than real-world dictators. ... Policy makers who have forgotten Orwell's lessons are ... creating government databases containing information about private citizens." According to Singleton, Big Brother is here with us now, not in the form of video surveillance at department stores, but in government departments gathering real information about its citizens.

Sandra Bullock's movie, "The Net" is the fictional story of Amanda Bennet, whose identity was retrieved from the 'system' and altered. Although this is Hollywood, it's a feasible scenario in today's world. We already have invasive security measures. Children born in Australia obtain a number when their parents register for family payments. "Centrelink", a conglomeration of the old Department of Social Security and Commonwealth Employment Service, allows the Australian Government to collect, store and cross-reference every personal detail of every Australian. Centrelink takes this unique number and liaises with the Australian Tax Office to cross-reference an individual's data. This concept of an all-knowing department is the very idea Australians resoundingly rejected in 1986. Bob Hawke's "Australia Card" was the deposed vehicle, yet a scant two years later, the Government expanded the use of the tax file number, giving it the power to do exactly what the Australia Card proposed.

July 2000 in Australia saw the formation of CrimTrac, a policing agency organised to aid investigation of criminal matters. CrimTrac is accountable to the Department of the Attorney-General and was set up as a resource for the different States and Territories. On the surface, this is a step forward in criminal investigations, allowing police to tap into databases, cut down on investigation time and allow for conclusive evidence in the solving of complex crimes. However, with the formation of any database comes the possibility of misuse and abuse. CrimTrac is seeking permission to allow compulsory DNA testing of children at birth, and will store results on a 'secure' database. Australia's Federal Privacy Commissioner, Malcolm Crompton recognises that "storing this sensitive data on a criminal database has the very real potential to undermine our civil liberties by eroding our privacy." The notion of taking DNA samples from newborn babies is a violation of the legal code, which presumes innocence until guilt is proven. Crompton is calling for submissions from the public regarding this issue.

Crompton also points out a very real side issue - that of the security of sensitive personal data. He says, "In the current environment, there is little chance that such a sensitive genetic database could be secure enough to absolutely guarantee that the information would not be able to be used to frame people for crimes, or for other unrelated purposes." Following the murder of Janelle Patton on Norfolk Island in early 2002, the Australian Federal Police combined with the Norfolk Police to solve the crime - to no avail. Then in August, they announced a voluntary fingerprint taking program in an effort to reach a breakthrough. Norfolk residents would be asked to submit to fingerprinting with the understanding that their fingerprints would only be used to solve the Ms Patton's murder and would be destroyed following the successful solving of that mystery. While it is certain this is the intended use of the fingerprints, it is also highly probable the information could be leaked and the information used for other purposes. We simply do not have sufficient security systems to guarantee such sensitive information remains in "the right hands" and is used for the "right purposes".

However, databases of known criminals serve their purpose. Cases are solved much easier by utilising databases containing identifiers, such as fingerprints, DNA, vehicle registration, and previous criminal history. However, many cases remain unsolved because the perpetrator is not known, and has no previous criminal record. Knowing there is a database which could pin a crime on someone doesn't stop crime. Similarly, a database with known terrorists isn't going to stop someone from choosing that course, if they so desire.

But governments are not only creating databases of known criminals. In 2002, the Queensland Government introduced new laws which will create a database of law-abiding citizens. Adults wishing to work with children, either on a voluntary or paid basis, need to register. After passing extensive police and background checks, they will be issued a card stating their suitability to care for children. Presumably a card-carrying volunteer will not molest or harm children. Thorough background checks will not prevent a previously unconvicted paedophile, or child molester from obtaining a card. This will grant him or her license to continue their activities under a cloak of respectability. Parents supervising their own children in activities involving other children are exempt. Evidence suggests parents may also abuse or molest children. Inclusion on a database of non-paedophiles creates for the 'un-caught' criminal an aura of respectability and gives children and their parents a false sense of security.

Collecting baby's DNA at birth erodes our freedom. Databases of personal information sold to insurance companies and marketing agencies erodes our freedom, and a database of 'child-safe' adults with no prior conviction of child abuse doesn't secure our children's lives. Without freedom we have no security. Freedom doesn't mean a lack of law and order but it does suggest the rights of individuals to pursue interests and abilities within a legal framework. Freedom to choose implies freedom to accept the consequences of choice, and this applies to our freedom to choose tougher security measures. In the light of September 11, we could accept greater security at airports. However, carry-on baggage in Australian airports is already scanned. Passengers walk through metal detectors. Sniffer dogs search for drugs, and random searches are routinely conducted of personal luggage.

New databases and ever-tightening government-sponsored security measures are not the answer. The answer lies in individuals taking back the responsibility for their own personal security. And for this to be viable, individuals need to be educated as to what those rights are, and the responsibilities that accompany them. This education needs to come from the private sector. Allowing governments to continue to educate its citizens is endorsing the power governments already have.

For too many years, people have been content to allow governments power over their lives. Singleton says, "when we rely on the federal government to solve our problems, we invite it to intrude upon our privacy; we are asking Big Brother to come in and make himself at home." We can and should change this. While a full-scale insurrection is neither warranted nor desirable, there are numerous avenues open to the individual to protect his or her rights and freedoms and the rights and freedoms of those for whom they are responsible.

The technology is already out there. Educating the population regarding its existence and uses will unlock the door to greater freedoms and individual self-control. Some technology needs refining and most can be adapted for personal needs. The use of fingerprint or retina scans to allow private entry into their own homes, offices and safes is one example. However to be a viable option, costs must be kept down. There is no need to involve government agencies in securing your premises. If premises were secure, there would be no property crime and the government would have no need for a DNA database to match against possible perpetrators.

Another possible solution would be the re-arming of the citizenry to allow upstanding citizens to defend their rights. Although there are many pros and cons for such an argument, the fact remains that in many American states where gun control is relaxed or non-existent, crime is low. In Australia where guns are fiercely controlled, violent crimes using firearms are still common. Even with a database of licensed gun owners, many perpetrators of violent crimes still go unpunished. Often while police go through this list of known gun owners, real criminals elude them and are long gone. Neither they nor their guns appear on it. Allowing the citizens to bear arms also helps to protect the nation against intruders as was in the case of the Great War when the "man on the land" took his rifle and joined with the existing force to defend his country. This engenders national pride and allows individuals to protect what is theirs to protect - the rights and privileges of living in a free country. Perhaps these freedoms were taken for granted and we've lost them to government legislation and bureaucracy. Yet the spirit is still strong. The Flight 93 passengers of September 11 took the matter in their own hands and defended their country as best they could.

Do we want a "Big Brother" society where controllers know our every move? Keep privacy matters sacred. No child needs their DNA on record. A database of law-abiding citizens does not protect the innocence of youth. This is reality, not Hollywood, and reality dictates freedom. We must not trade our fragile freedoms for more Government-style security. We must not give more power to our governments. If we learn anything from the aftermath of September 11, it should be this: Governments often know of disastrous events before they happen, but <u>do not</u>, or <u>cannot</u> act to prevent the disaster. It's up to us. We must utilise the available technology, fund research into greater security technologies to protect individual privacy and educate the people to return the power to them. Big Brother might be knocking on our doors; we <u>must not</u> let him in.

August 2002

Point of View: It's all relative, really

I HAD A DREAM …

"How Do You Define Earth Ethics, and How Would You Apply that Definition In Your Daily Life?"

It was the beginning of the new Millennium.

That night I had a dream. I lived in a beautiful world where Humans and Nature lived together in a true symbiosis. We tended the Earth with respect and love, taking only what was needed, nourishing the Earth and repairing minor damages as they occurred. The Earth repaid our kindness by giving freely of her abundance. Earth blossomed and all creatures lived in peace. It was paradise.

I awoke to the smell of gunpowder, as New Year's Eve celebrations reached a climax with fireworks and three reports from a rifle. I held my breath in stunned silence as, in the name of fun, would-be revellers let loose another barrage of human noise, pollution and aggression. I could almost feel Earth's pounding heartbeat as she slowly recovered from yet another shock. She seemed old and tired. Her sighs touched my soul as my own heartbeat returned to normal.

According to the Holy Bible, a command to care for the Earth was given to Adam and Eve while they were in the Garden of Eden. They, and by implication, the entire human race, were commanded to "Be fruitful, and multiply, and replenish the earth, and subdue it and have dominion over the fish of the sea, and over the fowl of the air, and over every living thing that moveth upon the earth." [1]

This summarises Earth Ethics. God charged all humanity with the mandate to take control of the earth. Having dominion over every living creature doesn't imply a position of tyranny and wastefulness. Rather, the direction was a loving one of caring for, using wisely and beautifying the earth.

Whether plants, animals, minerals, or even the earth itself, can be said to be sentient, and express feelings is immaterial. It is our stewardship, and our responsibility. Each human is accountable for the state of the earth. The direction bestowed upon us by God, to care for and tend the earth, is proof of His high regard for nature. It is therefore our duty to follow His direction, and care for our planet.

A misinterpretation of that passage of scripture has seen gross negligence on the part of our

---

[1] Genesis 1:28 (Authorised King James Version)

forebears, a legacy perpetuated by many today. Francis Bacon proposed that nature was something to be conquered.[2] It would appear that since the time Adam and Eve left the Garden and began to multiply and replenish the earth, their progenitors have proceeded to conquer. In modern times the search for ease, comfort and entertainment has spawned factories to produce textiles and other commodities whose specific purpose is to create more leisure time with less time spent in menial labour.

Rather than produce our own food, we rely on supermarkets to provide food grown on vast acres of land, ploughed, planted, poisoned with chemicals and reaped in a virtually never-ending cycle. We breed animals to stock butcher shops and supermarket shelves. How many die a wasted death due to an oversupply to the market? How much wasted produce rots on wharves and railway sidings because they cannot be sold, while millions of people starve? How many trillions of acres of native forest the world over is cleared to make room for cash crops, grazing land for cattle, and wooden trinkets and furniture created more for decoration than utility?

The problem today is the consumer mentality of most of the world's population. Tom Jay, "an artist, wordsmith and leader in the effort to restore salmon habitat" reminds us that to "consume" means, "to destroy utterly".[3] Utter destruction is not the end we

---

[2] Rev. Paul Peterson, Christian Bio-Ethics, Lecture Ten

[3] Larry Parks Daloz, Earth Ethics, A conversation with Larry Rassmussen at the Whidbey Institute

visualize for either ourselves, or the earth on which we live. Yet this is the road we are rapidly travelling. Scientists believe a large extra-terrestrial rock ended the life of the dinosaurs on earth. It was a cataclysmic event they had no power to forestall. The path we are on is no less catastrophic.

We, however, do have the power to avert disaster. Rev. Paul Peterson claims that "for humans to act in a way that leads to self-destruction" can only be described as "sheer stupidity and audacity" and destroying multitudes of other species along the way is irresponsible.[4] The responsible human agrees. With the great technological knowledge available to us, there is no excuse for the ostrich mentality. "The truth is out there" to quote the X-Files and is not even hidden. We need only heed the warning, and act.

I believe the damage must be repaired on the individual scale, but the decision must be unanimous. Many City councils provide kerbside recycling programmes. These are only the beginning. In a small city block with little garden area, our family is limited to what we can do. Restricting water usage and caring for this precious resource is our major contribution to caring for the planet. Using Earth-friendly phosphate-free detergents is essential as used water is returned to the system. Over-watering, sprinkling in the heat of the day, and other inappropriate watering methods are wasteful, and do more harm than good.

---

[4] Rev. Paul Peterson, Christian Bio-Ethics, Lecture Ten

Choosing products for their minimal packaging is another contribution we make. Some products are over-wrapped in the name of brand-identification, however with growing awareness, companies are changing their wrapping habits, even choosing to utilise recycled paper products. Choosing these nature-conscious products shows our support for the efforts these companies make for the environment.

We also re-use plastic shopping bags. They're used for rubbish disposal, of course, but this year our Christmas wreath will be made from twenty cut and tied bags, inexpensive recycled trinkets, and a tired coat hanger! Not only is it inexpensive, but also a crafty use for what is otherwise an environmental disaster.

Ultimately, it's not how much we do for the environment that counts. Education counts. If knowledge isn't passed on, any effort is vain. For this reason, I teach my children to care for their Earth. It is the only one we have, and they will inherit it.

Bibliography

The Holy Bible, Authorised King James Version

Peterson, Rev. Paul, 1999 **Christian Bio-Ethics, Lecture Ten, Earth Ethics**, http://www.bighole.com/church/earthetics.htm, Accessed 28/12/00.

Daloz, Larry Parks, Earth Ethics, A conversation with Larry Rassmussen at the Whidbey Institute,

http://www.whidbeyinstitute.org/discuss_ee.html. Accessed 28/12/00.

November 2001

Point of View: It's all relative, really

Phoebe Wilby

ABOUT THE AUTHOR

Originally from Australia, Phoebe now lives in West Yorkshire with her husband Ewen and two of her five children.

She has always loved the written word – but couldn't tell you who her favourite author is. She doesn't have just one! She reads anything from cereal packets through historical romances to Sci-Fi / Fantasy, and pretty much anything in between. She discovered Tolkien in her early twenties and more recently has read JK Rowling's Harry Potter series (a couple of times) and Stephenie Meyer's Twilight series. She even went through a crime stage, reading Nora Roberts and Patricia Cornwell, as well as a horseracing phase with Dick Francis. Basically, if it had words, she'd read it!

Her earliest childhood memories of writing include a ghost story she wrote in Year 4 and a humorous story involving her head teacher's fear of thunderstorms in Year 6. Sadly she no longer has copies of these and would have loved to revisit them to see how her style has developed over the years. She is working on a couple of novels, but has yet to finish them. In the meantime she offers this collection of short stories, poetry and essays.

Printed in Great Britain
by Amazon